TH

Kate Starling wa ... sherbet out of a cardboard carton.

"Mmmm," she said, lick-licking the spoon. She turned on the stool, bringing her thighs into contact with mine. Her robe parted and I caught a glimpse of where her tan line ended. She saw me looking and smiled. My head felt very thick, like I was swathed in cotton.

"When you're doing your fish guide gig, some of your clients must be in the money," she said, placing her hands on my knees and squeezing. "What I'm suggesting, Stash, is that you could do yourself a favor."

The hands on my knees slid higher as she leaned forward. "Any investor you bring in, you'd get a commission. You can take it in shares or in cash."

"Let's talk about it later," I said, drawing her to me. This time her hands slipped under my shirt. The tips of her fingers stroked over my chest.

Playing with Kate Starling was playing with dynamite — no matter what kind of bang you got out of it. . . .

THE CRYSTAL BLUE PERSUASION

W. R. PHILBRICK

AN ONYX BOOK

NEW AMERICAN LIBRARY

PUBLISHER'S NOTE

This book is a work of fiction. Names, characters, places, and incidents either are the product of the author's imagination or are used fictitiously, and any resemblance to actual persons, living or dead, events, or locales is entirely coincidental.

Copyright © 1988 by W.R. Philbrick

 Onyx is a trademark of New American Library.

SIGNET, SIGNET CLASSIC, MENTOR, ONYX, PLUME, MERIDIAN and NAL BOOKS are published by NAL PENGUIN INC., 1633 Broadway, New York, New York 10019

First Printing, February, 1988

1 2 3 4 5 6 7 8 9

PRINTED IN THE UNITED STATES OF AMERICA

For the citizens of the Conch Republic,
and for Dudley Frasier, of Manhattan

1

NEVER MIND what Noël Coward said about Englishmen, it's mad dogs and Key West fishermen who go out in the noonday sun. Take it from a native—your typical conch will chase fish anytime of day or night, in any kind of weather. Blame it on cheap rum, or the salt in our blood, the fact is when we see a tarpon showing its tail something deeper than dreams takes over: *Delirium fishies.*

That was my excuse for risking *Bushwhacked* with a hurricane offshore and the barometer free-falling. Mutt Durgin thought it was a dumb idea, and said so.

"I been tryin' to get you off your duff for most of the month of August," he said, chawing at the stub of his cigar. "Had to turn away two Texans and a Montana millionaire because the laziest fishing guide in the Lower Keys would rather swing in his hammock than earn an honest day's pay. and now you're going out free of charge to chase a herd of dumb-ass pilot whales? With a ten-foot swell breaking over the reef? You mind telling me why?"

"Because they asked me," I said, pulling Mutt out of his bait shack. "And you're going to help."

With me pushing and wheedling and making a nuisance, we headed out to the end of Mutt's wharf where *Bushwhacked*, my little skiff, was gassed and ready to go. The hot, still air smelled of mangroves and rotting baitfish. The sea had that glassy, deceptively calm look it gets when bad weather is coming. On the other side of the basin the big shrimpers were rafted three deep, warped and sprung to ride out a blow. Mutt squinted, wrinkling his forehead as he worried the unlit cigar.

While I steered *Bushwhacked* through the basin, Mutt broke out the life jackets, handing me one without comment. A glance from his pale, sun-shot eyes was reproach enough. Inside the breakwater at Fleming Key sailors were swarming over the navy hydrofoil, lashing the odd-looking beast to the concrete piers. The last time Key West took a direct hit from a killer hurricane Fleming Key didn't even exist, so there was no way of knowing how the vessels sheltering there would ride if the big wind decided to come ashore at full scream. Maybe the riprap and the tons of fill would hold. Maybe not.

"Got a match?"

Mutt was grinning around a fresh cigar. Brown and weather-beaten and as bald as a speckled egg, Mutt claims to be a swamp cracker from the Everglades, but when he gets excited a funny twang slips into his voice, the kind of diphthong you hear along the Jersey Shore. I've given up quizzing his past because he never tells the same lies twice. All I know is, when Mutt first showed up in Key West he had a gold hoop in his ear and some hair on his head and a mangy parrot that rode his shoulder. He used to pose in Mallory Square for camera-clicking tourists—for a fee, of course—until the parrot up and died. Or got eaten by a pet gator, depending on how he tells it. Whatever, Mutt leases a section of wharf now, where he runs a combination bait shop and fuel dock and books clients for no-account skiff guides like yours truly.

"Where these whales at, Stash?"

"Smathers Beach," I said.

Bushwhacked uncurled a green wake as we left the channel and cut through the shallow waters of Florida Bay. Mutt puffed fiercely at the cigar, which I happened to know had never cleared customs. Borders are amorphous down here in the keys, as easily crossed, almost, as the median line on a highway. Hence the brisk trade in contraband, ranging from Cuban cigars and Caribbean rum to bales of reefer madness and, lately, Columbian flake by the ton. Native conchs (rhyme it with "honks") are as tough as the shellfish they're named for, and have long considered smuggling a laudable career option. The feds are opposed to that line of endeavor, needless to say, and invest a lot of time and money trying to discourage it.

I'd been in the business myself, briefly, and got out one step ahead of the guard with the big iron key. Now it was the straight life for T.D. Stash—or as near as I can make it. Now and then I stray, although not to running bales or nose candy. What I do is, sometimes I help someone in a way that isn't strictly legal. For the right person and the right reason I'm willing to stroll into that much-disputed Gray Area just outside the law that gives good cops migraines and makes bad lawyers rich. If things work out—they don't always—I'm suitably rewarded for services rendered. The extra income means I can take time off from fish guiding to lie in my hammock reading Conrad or, as the whim takes me, help dissuade pilot whales from suiciding on Smathers Beach.

"This marine biologist who called you," Mutt shouted over the noise of the hundred-and-forty-horse outboard. "It an attractive female-type biologist, by any chance?"

He had me there. I was all for saving the whales,

but Dr. Lauren Ashby, a long-legged, sun-drenched redhead gave the enterprise a certain, well, urgency. I'd never had anything going with Dr. Ashby, although I wasn't exactly opposed to the notion. Far from it. More than a few of the daydreams I'd entertained while hammock-bound had involved her and me in close proximity.

"Wipe that look off your face," I said to Mutt. "Hang on, we're going to hit some chop!"

Emerging from the calm waters in the lee of Stock Island, the change was immediate and violent. As *Bushwhacked* slammed into the ragged seas I lowered the throttle hastily. A blast of spray tore the cigar from Mutt's face. He laughed and grabbed hold of the rail while I puzzled over how best to approach the beach without getting swamped. The swells were short and steep, just nasty enough to be worrisome. Using the airport tower as a point of reference, and with Mutt's demented laughter as encouragement, I managed to bring *Bushwhacked* ashore without taking too much paint off the bottom.

The army of volunteers Lauren Ashby had recruited came in all sexes, shapes, sizes, and hairstyles: aging hippies, drifters, conchs, and students from the community college where she lectures. Most of the volunteers were waist-deep in the warm water, trying to hold the massive pilot whales off the beach. Lauren, wearing a black maillot swimsuit, was coordinating the effort: shouting instructions and encouragement, laying on hands, helping to sponge the beached whales.

"It's their weight," she said, crouching next to a gasping calf. "They get exhausted or confused, they want to come in and take a rest, but out of water their mass is too much, they don't have enough strength to fill their lungs. So what they do, they lay here and smother."

She said it matter-of-factly. The good doctor was a realist. Pilot whales, like certain two-legged mammals, have an inexplicable tendency towards self-destruction. It seems to be their nature. There was only so much Ashby could do. She and her ragged brigade might, by brute strength, push the lolling beasts into deeper water, but there was no way to reprogram their sense of direction or erase the beaching impulse.

"This time we can blame it on the storm," she said, walking Mutt and me back to where we'd nudged *Bushwhacked*'s bow into the sand. "Last time it was the moon, or the stars, or something they ate. The sad thing is, nobody knows *what* makes them do it."

I was disappointed when she didn't seem to notice me noticing the fine way her body moved inside the slick swimsuit. Which made me think she was more interested in my skiff than me.

"What I had in mind," Lauren said, "you could sort of play shepherd with your boat. My people are doing a pretty good job keeping them off the shore, but once we get them pointed in the right direction they tend to wander back. Some of it is the swells, I assume. If we can get them out beyond where it breaks, they might have a chance."

It was tricky business and I am damn glad Mutt was along for the ride. He handled the pole, gently prodding the whales, while I handled the boat.

"What was the name of that movie?" he said, hefting the blunt pole like a harpoon. "*Moby Dick*, right? Only they didn't mess around with anything this small."

"Small" was between fifteen and twenty-five feet, plenty big enough for me, and almost more than the boat could handle. As Dr. Ashby had surmised *Bushwhacked* was relatively easy to maneuver in shallow water and the fiberglass push-pole was handy for fending off denizens of the deep. Not that we didn't have problems. Keeping a herd of heavy, seagoing mammals in line would have been difficult even in calm waters. The steep swells made it tough, sometimes dangerous. Two thousand pounds of blubber and bone will rattle your teeth pretty good when it bumps under the keel.

When a frisky pilot nudged us, Mutt lost his balance and went over the side, clutching the pole like a falling Wallenda. After a swell passed he popped up in the shallow water and shook himself like wet bird dog.

"Sum bitch!" he sputtered. "This is better'n bein' drunk!"

The *Citizen* reported that of sixty-three whales, fifty had been directed to open water, while thirteen were stranded and died, despite the best efforts of Dr. Ashby and her volunteers. At the time I wasn't counting. When the swells seemed to lessen in the late afternoon—the latest weather bulletin said the front was stalled—we took our chance. I cut behind the stragglers, sweeping left to right, leaving the throttle wide. The herd began to act less listless, more interested in forward progress. Picking up speed, their sleek black bodies rolled through the green water. They were a noisy bunch, clicking and bellowing and blowing air. No manners at all.

When we cleared Whitehead Spit a crowd of locals gave us a cheer from the grounds of the old fort. As if aware of all the fuss they'd caused, the whales began cavorting in the deep water of the Southwest Channel. I cut back on the throttle. The herd kept moving, heading for the opening in the reef.

Mutt, exhausted, lay propped up in his yellow life jacket, muttering about do-gooders.

"I guess it don't hurt to do something right once in a while," he said. "I ain't gonna make a habit of it, though."

When we got back to the wharf, Lily Cashman was waiting in the bait shack. She wore loose cotton shorts and a pastel-green blouse knotted at her waist. Her bare feet rested on a crab trap. A pair of Kino sandals poked out of her string purse.

"Okay, hotshot," she said, tipping her sunglasses up. "How about helping out us humans?"

Lil had that pouty, lawyerish look she gets when she's determined to make life difficult for someone.

"Come on," she said. "I'll buy you a beer. Dinner, too. You name it."

That meant trouble.

2

LILY CASHMAN perched on a corner stool at the Half Shell Bar, where we had a view of the basin and the turtle kraals. The air-conditioned breeze blowing through the restaurant felt good, although it made me aware of the sweat evaporating from my T-shirt. Lil tapped her painted fingernails and sighed.

"It's Sammie," she said. "She's done it again."

Lil is slim and trim. She has auburn hair going sun-blond at the ends, lime-green eyes, and a faint spray of freckles over the bridge of her nose. In my opinion she's the best-looking attorney in the Lower Keys. That cuts no ice with Lil. Her heart belongs to Samantha, who has a tattoo to prove it. I assumed Sammie had run off, or taken another lover. It had happened before, but Lil laughed at the suggestion.

"No way," she said. "We're tight right now. Tighter than we've ever been."

"Glad to hear it."

"What happened, Sammie got conned out of ten thousand dollars."

I whistled. Sammie ran a Windsurfer concession at the public beach. It was a risky business, dependent on tourism and weather. Ten grand was more than she could hope to clear for an entire season. Most of the money, Lil explained, came not from the rental profits, but from her mother's estate.

"The old lady had this house up in Naples, no

mortgage, property tax was manageable. She figures she'll be leaving Samantha pretty well fixed, when the time comes. Then the cancer starts eating her up and the medical bills eat up her equity even faster. After the estate paid out there was a little more than nine thousand left over. What I wanted Sam to do was put it in a long-term savings account, or maybe bonds. Bonds would have been fine."

"Sammie isn't the bonds type, Lil. Bonds are boring."

The bartender brought me a beer. I swallowed some, washing the salt out of my throat. Trade was slow at the Half Shell Raw Bar. In peak season, when the snowbirds hit town, the customers would be lined up outside the door and into the parking lot. Now there were empty tables and the only steadies were local wharf rats like me.

"Let me guess," I said. "She got suckered in a condo scheme."

Lil sipped at her strawberry daiquiri. "Worse," she said. "She gave it to Harper King, as in King-Ducat Salvors, Inc."

"Are you serious?"

"I am. But King isn't. Not about the salvage business," she said. The strawberry juice stained her lips blood-red. "What he's serious about is taking money from girls who should know better."

I nodded. "And you'd like me to go see old Harper and ask him pretty please if he'll give the money back."

"Whatever it takes," she said, grinning like a vampire. "Use your imagination."

You don't leave the hammock all at once. Not in the dog days of August in the south of Florida. Not when there's still a few bucks in the checking account and twenty-six pages to go in *Typhoon*. Not if you're as prudent and careful and lazy as yours truly. So after sharing a plate of conch fritters with Lily Cashman, I finished my second beer and ambled through the sleepy streets of Old Town, heading back to Hammockville.

The bungalow where I make my home is a small, one-story job, built of cinder block laid on a slab. It has cool tile floors and ceiling fans. In back there's a screened-in porch that overlooks a very small yard and a very large ficus tree that has more vines than Tarzan. The porch is where I rig my hammock. Suspended there in the humid darkness, I listened to the palmetto bugs crash against the screens and thought about the melancholia of whales and marine biologists in black swimsuits. A Spanish-inflected voice on the radio announced that the first hurricane of the season was stalled five hundred miles to the southeast. Rain was expected. A few drops dinged the tin roof. I decided that remaining horizontal was brilliant strategy.

I would, of course—eventually—attempt to recover Sammie's ten grand. I owed Lil that much. My summer of leisure was the result, largely, of a lucrative spouse-recovery her firm had steered my way: a frightened, drug-dependent hubbie on the run from domestic and legal problems. I located him in a roach-infested trailer on Stock Island, shacked up with an ounce of bad coke. Once it was explained that all was forgiven, he was more than willing to leave the fetid little box on wheels and go home to face the music. No muss, no fuss, no silly games with guns—from my point of view a perfect piece of work.

It rained all night—a hard, drenching downpour. I

slept in the hammock and dreamt I was a sailor in a tin boat chasing small blue fish over an azure sea. When dawn broke, the empty streets were steaming and there were high thin clouds moving through sky.

I bought a double Cuban coffee from Mr. Sánchez and sat on the bench in front of his bodega, drank the coffee, and read *Solares Hill*, the underground monthly. The *Solares Hill* freelancers had been following the exploits of Harper King and his King-Ducat Salvors operation with lively interest. And no wonder. A treasure hunt, real or phony, was a welcome change from the usual drug busts and real-estate swindles. The article raised a lot of pertinent questions. Would King be the next Mel Fisher? Would he, too, find a motherlode of Spanish gold? Did Harper King really have a claim on the site of a wrecked galleon? Was King, described as "charismatic," really after reef-strewn treasure, or was he just another con man with a fancy boat and a line of jive for gullible investors? The reporter filing the stories didn't draw any conclusions, but gave the impression she would like to believe in King, if only because he happened to be only long-running story in a slow, rainy season. No mention was made of the ten grand he'd promoted from Sammie, but then it wasn't the sort of transaction either side was likely to want publicized.

The strong Cuban coffee gave me courage. I decided the best way to help Lily and Sam was to turn myself in to the police. The officer at the desk squinted at me. I think he disapproved of my ratty sneakers, cutoff jeans, and ventilated T-shirt.

"I'm here to confess," I said. "Please inform Lieutenant Kerry."

The cop looked wary. He knew my face but couldn't quite place me.

"Your name?" he asked.

"Ted Bundy."

He frowned and told me not to move. I disobeyed, flopping into a chair after he left the front desk. A few minutes later the lieutenant poked his head out, sighted me, and grimaced.

"Come along, Mr. Bundy," he said. "I was just plugging in your chair."

When I was in the fifth grade my best friend was a skinny, freckle-faced kid named Nelson Kerry. We traded baseball cards and comic books and imagined we would grow up to be ballplayers or superheroes. Nelson grew up to be a cop—Lieutenant Detective Nelson Kerry of the Key West Police Department, to be exact. I grew up to be an unlicensed trouble-maker. We long ago ceased to be close friends. Mostly, I think, because old Nelly is afraid he'll really have to arrest me one of these days.

In his office Kerry pointed at the coffee machine and put his feet up on his desk. When I declined the coffee he offered a stick of gum.

"You're off the butts," I said.

"I thought you were Ted Bundy the psycho-killer," he said. "Now I guess you're the Amazing Kreskin, reading my thoughts."

"You never chew gum unless you've just quit smoking."

"I went up to Islamorada to this hypnotist they got up there, supposed to be a real genius."

"It work?"

"Nah, I drive out of there, reach into the glove compartment, and I've got one lit up before I know what I'm doing. Never tasted so good. Fifty bucks, right? Pack of gum sets me back forty cents, works better." The lieutenant dropped his feet to the floor and showed me his teeth as he masticated the gum.

"I got this feeling, T.D., you didn't drop in to ask me how was it going, my twenty-third attempt to give up cigarettes."

I told him about Sammie investing ten grand in King-Ducat Salvors and wanting it back.

Kerry got a funny look in his eye. He took the gum from his mouth, wrapped it in a piece of foil, and dropped it in the waste bin. "What's your angle, T.D.? You know something about Harper King that makes you think he's not on the level?"

"Only what I read in the papers."

"Yeah? Well, now. I been reading the same paper you all have and I don't recall it said anything about a bunco operation."

I put my hand up. "Whoa, Nellie," I said. "I'm not accusing King of fraud. I'm just asking if you've heard anything on the grapevine. What's the problem? Is the guy a friend of yours?"

The lieutenant settled down. "I met him a couple times. Over the Havana Docks. He's got—Stash, I'm not exaggerating—he's got the most outrageous girlfriend. Really spectacular. I'm having a couple of pops in there one night, naturally I attempt to engage the lady in conversation. Harp comes back from the men's, or wherever, he immediately picks up on it."

"Gosh," I said. "And you a sworn officer of the law."

"I said, 'Excuse me, my mistake.' Believe me, I'm ready to move on. He's not a bad-looking guy, Harper King, reminds me of one of those old-time movie stars like what's-his-name, Clark Gable. You know, a funny little mustache and big ears. Only he's built like a gorilla, must go two-forty, most of it muscle. I start to get off the bar stool, he grabs me around the shoulders. What he wants to do is buy me a drink. He's giving me a hug, just being friendly."

"He didn't notice you trying to hustle the girl."

Kerry unwrapped another piece of gum and chewed it thoughtfully. "Sure he noticed. He just found it amusing. Harp tells me, any man who doesn't make a pass at Kate—that's her name, Kate—is either out of his mind, gay, or dead. Maybe all three."

"So," I said, "other than your approval of the women he attracts, what's your impression of Harper King?"

Kerry shrugged. He looked out the window, where a coconut palm was in the act of shedding a dead frond. "My impression," he said, "is I like the guy."

"Is he on the level?" I asked. "Is King-Ducat a good investment?"

"Know what?" the lieutenant said. "You're the only sunnova bitch I know comes in here and gets away with grilling me like this. Usually the way it works, I only answer questions when they got me in court."

"I'm pushy," I said. "But I'm lovable."

"Okay, you want my gut reaction? Gut reaction is that Harper King is straight. What I can see, he's spending a lot of dough on the salvage operation. He's got that monster boat to take care of. If he's skimming off the investors, it's not obvious how he's doing it."

"Nelson," I said, "you've been checking him out."

"Sure," he said. "In an unofficial capacity. I haven't had a look at his books, if that's what you mean. Whether it's a good investment, I wouldn't know. You buy shares in a salvage operation, a wreck you don't even know exactly where it is, that has to be a risky investment. Which, by the way, Harp is the first to say so."

"How's business?" I said. "Is he selling a lot of shares? Raising enough capital?"

"No idea," Kerry said. "They've got this booth on the corner Duval and Front Street where they pass out brochures, like the real-estate people do. There's this video presentation he gives and anybody who wants to can go aboard *Ducat* and check out the operation. How many of those people actually invest, I don't know."

"Sammie did."

"Yeah."

"And one other person we both know."

It had been a long time since I'd seen Nelson Kerry blush. My guess about his investing in King-Ducat Salvors was on the mark.

"I don't know what it is about you T.D. You come in here and ask me what I think of Harp and right away I'm embarrassed maybe I got suckered. Now, why is that?"

"Look, Nel, for all I know he's straight as an arrow."

"Yeah, but just the fact that you're snooping around gets me worried. Only what have I got to lose, the worst happens? Twenty-five hundred bucks? That's a month's pay, before they take out the taxes. They don't recover any goodies, or Harp skips with the dough, I'm only out a month's pay."

"Right," I said, wanting to be agreeable. "You can't get hurt."

"Mel Fisher is down here, what—fifteen years? Every year or so he finds a few cannon, or a couple buckets of doubloons, or those silver bars. Any idiot can figure he's on the level, that sooner or later he'll find the motherlode if it's out there. Any every year I'd think about buying a share, just for the hell of it. Take a chance."

"Only you didn't."

"Exactly right. So one day Mel Fisher finds *Atocha*

and pretty soon he's dividing up millions with the shareholders who had guts enough to buy a piece of the excitement and I'm down there on the dock, making sure none of the new millionaires double-park."

"This time you want in."

Kerry snapped the gum. "What the hell," he said. "I figure I look good in gold."

3

FROM MALLORY Square, the salvage vessel *Ducat* looked like a cruise ship. At a hundred and twenty or so feet in length it wasn't quite large enough to qualify, but her designers had used a full bag of visual tricks to enhance a shiplike impression. Anchor chains were dumped like massive watch fobs on the big, sweeping bow. The scaled-down details of a liner were beautifully executed in the aluminum superstructure. The diesel exhaust stack was intentionally oversized, surmounted by a bristle of antennas, radar equipment, and a satellite navigation transponder. The effect was to suggest a mass and power the hull could not possibly have and still be able to navigate in the shallow waters surrounding the keys.

Top-heavy or not, she was a pretty thing, pleasing to the eye. I guesstimated her cost as about thirty-five grand a foot, by the time the extensive electronics were installed. Absurdly expensive yachts of her type and size, not uncommon up around Fort Lauderdale and Palm Beach, were less frequently seen in the Lower Keys. North or south, I'd never heard of one being rerigged as a salvage vessel. It was like converting a new Rolls for use in a demolition derby.

There were two people at work on the rear deck, loading scuba tanks into racks in an area that had once been, from the look of it, a small helipad. Nowadays every serious yachtsman wants to be able to land a chopper on deck. Useful for receiving harried executives and drug runners, two professions that are becoming increasingly blurred in this part of the world.

One of the deckhands was Billy Briggs. He was working bare-chested, showing off the bulging pectorals he'd developed up in the Raiford Correctional Facility. He didn't respond when I waved from the dock. No reason he should. I only knew Billy from his picture in the paper the time he brained a drinking buddy with a beer mug at a Stock Island dive. If I remembered correctly, he had done a deuce on a manslaughter charge. I hadn't seen him in the papers lately, so maybe he was keeping out of trouble.

"Nice little boat you've got there," I said. "Permission to come aboard?"

Briggs paused, a scuba tank suspended in his arms. With the blond brush cut and the Wayfarer shades he looked like an extra in a James Dean movie. All he needed was a toothpick.

He said, "We're kinda busy."

I was willing to lend a hand and said so. I took his shrug as tacit permission to board. When I got around to the stern, Briggs was slamming tanks into the rack. His deckmate, a slender, dark-haired girl of about twenty, introduced herself as Mindy. Outmuscled by at least sixty pounds, she was having trouble keeping up with Briggs and was more than willing to let me help. When all the tanks—three rows of twelve—were stowed, Briggs wiped his hands on the seat of his pants. He might have been staring me down. It was hard to tell with the shades hiding his eyes.

"Much obliged," he said, adding, "You ain't a tourist."

I agreed.

"I figured you was here to see Mr. King," he said, "about investing."

I allowed as I was not, unfortunately, a potential investor.

"See, the boss don't get back till tomorrow," Briggs said. "Got hisself delayed in Miami, on count of the weather."

I nodded. "You all looking for help?"

Briggs propped the Wayfarers on the bristles of his crew cut and squinted his small gray eyes. "Depends what kind," he said.

"Boat driver," I said. "Deckhand. Certified diver. All-thumbs mechanic."

Billy Briggs grinned. He had a lot of white teeth, evenly spaced. "I can always use a strong diver," he said. "You all a local boy, ain't ya?"

I didn't like being called a boy by a man several years my junior, but I nodded agreeably and introduced myself. "I fish-guide out of Dawson's Wharf," I said. "With the wet weather we been having, reservations have slacked off. I've done some wreck work. You need a reference, the local dive shops know me."

Briggs suggested we go below for a cold beer. Leaving, he ordered Mindy to scrub the deck with fresh water. She had the mop out was in the act of uncoiling the hose, but cheerfully agreed to proceed with what she had already begun. Used to taking orders from Admiral Briggs, was little Mindy.

"I'm the divemaster," Briggs said, leading me into a companionway. "Topside, Mr. King runs the show. Anything underwater, that's my department."

He took the long way down to the galley, showing off *Ducat*'s posh interior. Pointing out the teak-paneled salon, the sauna and Jacuzzi, the rec room, the workshop, storage holds, master suites, and crew quarters. Quoting prices that made me revise upward my original estimate of three million. All of which raised the question of why Harper King needed investors, if he owned a floating palace like *Ducat*. Samantha's ten grand wouldn't have paid for stereo equipment in the rec room, never mind the Waterford chandeliers in the grand salon.

Briggs clinked his beer bottle against mine. "Welcome aboard," he said. "Harp gets final approval, but he goes along with who I sign on, usually."

We sat in the salon, drinking beers and pretending we were just two good old boys who had stumbled onto a good thing. Anyhow, I pretended. It was hard to get a reading on Billy Briggs. Other than the bodywork, two years in Raiford didn't appear to have touched him. He had none of the typical jailbird mannerisms. I was beginning to wonder if I had him confused with somebody else when he brought the subject up.

"You might hear I killed a man," he said. "People do like to shoot their mouth about a thing like that. The truth is, I hit a friend of mine and he died. Accidental. Bein' as I was drunk, they sent me away. That's the long and short of it."

"None of my business."

"No, it ain't, but I'm telling you anyways 'cause you all bound to hear the X-rated version. That I was foolin' with the wife of the guy got killed. Which as it happen, I was. Didn't have nothing to do with the fight, though," Briggs said. "What happened, Lloyd had a soft head and I never knew it, or I sure as hell wouldn't a hit him."

Near as I could judge he was telling the truth, although I thought it might be prudent to duck if he ever lifted a beer mug. Changing from the interesting subject of adultery and murder, I asked what a diver might expect to be paid, were he to sign on.

"The way it is right now, there's a cash-flow problem. Costs an arm and a leg to take this tub outside the reef. So what Harp's been doing, he gives us all shares in the venture. A share goes for twenty-five hundred, you had to buy one. Also you'd get room and board and a hundred bucks a week spending money."

"How long you have to work to get a share?"

"A guy like you, knows his way around, about two weeks," Briggs said. "If old Harp likes your style, he liable to throw in a couple extra now and then. He's a very generous man."

Yes, indeed, very generous with pieces of paper. I asked Briggs what he thought the chances were of cashing in the shares.

He laughed. "Oh, man, you already got the bug, don't you? Well, all I can say, there's treasure down there. A couple tons of gold coin. Manifest shows silver bar, emeralds, stuff like that. Harp has all the documents. All we gotta do, we gotta find it, then we all be filthy rich."

"And if we don't?"

Billy Briggs grinned. "Then we still had us one fuck of a good time," he said. "I ain't gonna elaborate just yet, but you know what they callin' this here vessel?"

"Can't say I do."

"Call us *Loveboat*," he said. "And, bubba, that ain't no lie."

Mindy, finished with the rear deck, had transferred her attention to the teak cap rail. She was treating the wood with oil that smelled pungent and fresh. I tried not to watch her little bottom wiggle-waggle as she stroked the rail, but my eyes had a will of their own.

Obviously I was under the influence of the chauvinist Billy Briggs.

"You on the team?" she asked, buffing the wood-work.

"If Mr. King approves."

"You kidding?" Mindy's giggle made her sound even younger than she looked. "Harp likes every-body. If Billy wants you in, you're in."

The sky over the Gulf had been wiped clean by the overnight rain. Cirrus clouds were scudding to the east, drawing in clear, cooler air. For a few hours, at least, there was relief from the thick hu-midity of the season. I felt brand-new. It was barely noon and already I was on a treasure hunt of sorts.

"Let me guess," I said. "Ohio?"

"Michigan," Mindy said, handing me a buffing pad. "Little town called Elk Rapids."

Elk Rapids, it seemed, was a very small town on the shore of a great big lake. When Mindy left to visit her sister in Florida, the population declined to one thousand three hundred and twelve.

"I figure the luck will improve in Elk Rapids, now it's no longer double thirteen. Anyway, that's what I told my mom. I go, 'Momma, only way to change this number is I get pregnant or I go visit Sylvie in Sarasota.' That fixed her wagon."

I smiled. It was nice to know people still said "fix your wagon" in Elk Rapids, Michigan.

"Going to see Sylvie, that was just an excuse. I never been to Florida, see, never swum in warm ocean." Mindy paused to look over the side, where the sun made undulating pillars of light in the wa-ter. "I just love it, the way you can see right to the bottom. Back home you can't ever see so clear."

Back home in murky Lake Michigan was where Mindy had learned to dive. After the bone-crack cold and dark of the big lake, the tepid, teeming southern reefs were a dream come true. "Thing I could hardly believe, Sylvie and Don, that's her boyfriend, he cuts hair in the same salon she does, they won't hardly go in the water. They go down the beach, sure, but all they talk about is how there might be jellyfish, or sea urchins, or stingrays, you know, like that? I said to her, I go, 'Sylvie, come on, it's safe as churches. We're talking water temp of eighty degrees here, and if you're scared of stepping on something, wear your Reeboks, honey.' No way, she won't even go wading. Closest old Don comes to any marine life is when a little bit of the fishwich ends up in his french fries at MacDonalds.''

"Stop," I said. "You'll ruin my appetite."

"Barf me, huh? I'd rather eat rats, it comes to that. Well, Don, he's an okay guy, but after a couple weeks in that little trailer of theirs, I mean you'd have to be invisible not to wear out your welcome. Plus all they do is get high and watch dirty movies on the VCR. *Debbie Does Dallas*, I mean it's sort of funny for about five minutes, then you get this out-of-breath feeling.''

That was in June. The first week in July Mindy had packed up her gear and got on a bus and headed south until the road ended. She took a room at the Southern Cross Hotel, free-diving the reefs in the morning and looking for work in the afternoon.

"Everyone goes, this is the in-between season, honey. You can take your pick, come fall, but right now, uh uh, no way. I was down to about my last eight cents when Billy tried to pick me up at The Green Parrot.''

The way she described it, I could picture his swagger, hear his dull, confident spiel, smell the cheap schnapps on his breath. Making every effort to impress, Billy had bragged about his new position as divemaster aboard *Ducat*.

"First thing, I go, 'Is that the flash-looking boat tied up at Mallory Dock? The one looks like a millionaire must own it?' And right away Billy is just dying to give me the tour."

"I'll bet."

"Yeah, well, there's horny guys in Elk Rapids, too. But I know how to dance without getting my toes stepped on, if you know what I mean," she said. "So Billy brings me down here, figuring the 'tour' will start right in this cozy cabin where he's bunked. I had to go into this little gasping routine, say I had to get some fresh air topside or I might get the heaves. That cooled him out. So we go up top and Harp and Kate—that's Harp's girl, Kate Starling, she's really nice—they're having sundowners on the foredeck. I made Billy take me over and say hello and that's when I first mentioned I was a certified diver."

"And the rest is history."

Mindy went back to buffing the teak. "So far," she said.

A lemon-yellow Mercedes convertible pulled into the parking lot. It was a beautiful little machine and it came with a matching pneumatic blonde.

Mindy giggled. "That's Kate," she said. "Every guy, the first time he sees Kate, he gets that same look. Sort of dumb and hopeful."

"Huh?" I said.

"They get this dumb, hopeful look and make brilliant little quips like 'huh?' Happens every time. The thing kills me about Kate, if you have legs that long you should be about eight foot tall. Where she's just under six."

Just under six feet was plenty enough. I could see why Nelson Kerry had made a fool of himself at the Havana Docks Bar. Mindy plainly expected me to wag my tail and pant. Instead I concentrated on polishing the rail.

"Careful," she said. "That's only teak, that's meant to last a century. You rub any harder it'll disintegrate."

"Nobody likes a know-it-all."

"Not when Kate's around," she said, grinning impishly. "Out of her range, I do okay."

The lady in question tick-tocked up the gangway, carrying a plastic shopping bag. She was wearing crisp khaki culottes (try saying that three times fast), a tan sleeveless blouse, and deck shoes. Not that it mattered. Gunnysacks would have been just fine. She paused at the top of the gangway, said "Hi," and went directly inside.

Mindy said, "You can breathe now, Tarzan."

A brisk walk helped. I left Mindy to her polishing and did a quick march up Whitehead Street, counting cracks in the sidewalk. Cool out, Stash. Try to remember you're a grown man, not a hormone-crazed youth.

I went into The Green Parrot and drank a Coke quick enough so it burned on the way down. Then I put a coin in the juke and listened to Bing Crosby sing "White Christmas."

Better than a cold shower, old Bing.

4

LILY'S OFFICE is in a pink stuccoed building on the west end of Angela Street. The Christmas palms in the little front yard looked wilted when I scuffed my way up the tiled walk and through the open door.

"On the horn," Roger said, jerking his thumb at the louvered partition surrounding Lily's desk. "Oh," he said, glancing down at his typewriter. "This is for you."

I took the single-page form, backed through the opening in the partition, and dropped into the saggy wicker chair facing Lil, who was, as her secretary had implied, just getting off the phone.

"Hang a sign on me," I said." 'Gone fishing.' "

"What's that supposed to mean?"

"Means the fox has been invited into the hen-house."

Lily sighed. "Explain," she said.

I told her about hiring on as a diver. "I'm getting paid in shares," I said. "If things don't work out, Sammie and I can open an origami store."

"Don't talk dirty," Lily said, handing me a pen. "Besides, you're getting paid by me. Put your X at the bottom of that release."

"Can I read it first?"

"Only if you promise not to move your lips. Come on, T.D., it's the standard release I always have you sign."

"Which means you promise to pay me if I do what you want me to do—get the money back—and I promise not to hold you accountable if I get my ass in a sling."

Lily nodded. "I hate it when my friends sue me," she said. "It sours the relationship, you know?"

"I wouldn't know," I said. "What's a third of ten thousand?"

"For God's sake, sign it."

"This is going to be easy money, Lil," I said, making my scrawl. "This is going to be a piece of cake."

"Have all the cake you want," Lily said, putting the form in a file folder. "Just keep away from that blonde with all the legs."

"You make her sound like a centipede."

"I mean it, T.D. The lady is bad news."

On the way home I stopped at the bodega and had Mr. Sánchez assemble a Cuban mix special. I ate the sandwich at my kitchen table, right out of the waxed paper, and washed it down with a glass of milk. I figured the garlic on my breath would protect me from Kate Starling, the bad-news blonde.

After lunch I got my scuba gear from the storage bin, laid the equipment out on the living-room floor, and devoted two hours to a piece-by-piece inspection.

By the time I had the gear loaded up and delivered to Mallory Dock it was the cocktail hour. Party time. Amplified Jimmy Buffet blasted from the loudspeakers on deck. Strips of gold foil festooned the gangway and the door to the main salon. There was a buzz of conversation coming from inside, vying with the music. I took a deep breath and was about to crash the festivities when a voice hailed me from the companionway.

"Hey there, sailor, got a light?"

Mindy was wearing a strapless dress of enchantingly thin cotton. She had on eye makeup and tangerine lipstick. When she got closer I saw the fish lures dangling from her ears were really feathered earrings. She offered to help stow my duffel bags. "Harp's back," she said, nodding toward the salon. "Flew in with a bunch of Palm Beach investors. They're getting liquored up before the show starts."

"Show?"

"She grinned. "You'll see. Come on, let's get this gear down to the locker. Harp wants to meet his new diver. Show you off to the quality."

"I better go home and get my tux."

Mindy punched my arm. She had evidently decided we were good buddies, in a sibling sort of way. That was fine by me. The lockers were next to the dive station on the rear deck. Mindy gave me a brass padlock that had a key in it.

"Up to you," she said. "I lost the key to mine and had to hacksaw the hasp. Now what I figure, anyone wants to break in, the lock won't stop 'em."

"You keep a watch on this boat?" I asked.

"Not when we're docked here. When we're on site, sure. The drill is running lights on, anchor lights on, radar deflector up. Harp is pretty strict about that. Lot of traffic out there, especially after dark."

"Night fishing," I said.

"Right." Mindy smirked. "Since I got here we've been boarded twice by the Coast Guard. I guess what it is, they figure anything this big must be hauling bales."

"They find anything?"

She shook her head. The feathered earrings brushed her cheeks. "That's another thing Harp is pretty tight about. No dope on board."

I clinched the padlock and dropped the key in my

pocket. Someone clapped me between the shoulder blades, hard enough to make me catch my breath.

"Hey there, partner! Come on in and meet the boss."

Briggs had on crisp chinos and a new OP shirt. I looked down and saw new Top Sider deck shoes.

"Gosh, Bill, you been out shopping."

He laughed. "Kate got me this outfit. Wants her divemaster to make a good impression on the fat cats."

I glanced at my tattered sneakers and shook my head.

"You're fine," Briggs said. "Ain't he fine, Mindy?"

"He'll do," she said.

Not counting crew, there were fourteen guests in the main salon. Every last one appeared to be having one hell of a good time. And why not? King-Ducat Salvors had done it up proper, with a catered buffet, an open bar, and champagne I overheard one of the Palm Beach investors ·judge as "not too shabby." There was real money on board. You could hear it in the voices, see it in the choice of costume.

"I was wrong about the tux," I told Mindy. "What is required, my dear, is a pink blazer, silk ascot, and seersucker pants."

"What'd he say?" Briggs wanted to know.

"Said he's outclassed," Mindy said.

I snagged a glass of the bubbly from a passing tray as Mindy and Briggs steered me toward the center of attention. Himself, Harper King. He was, as my cop friend had implied, a big bear of a man. About my height, but larger all around, with an enormous chest and thick forearms. He was about forty, although the big ears and a freckled complexion gave him a boyish look that somehow was not diminished by a thinning hairline, clipped mustache, or the pronounced cleft in his chin. What Nelson Kerry had failed to mention was that Harper King had the mild blue eyes of a gentle giant; unless I was way off base, he was the type who would find it difficult to raise a fist in anger, despite his obvious size and strength.

When Billy introduced me, King's face creased in a smile, revealing a gold tooth.

"T. D. Stash," he said, pumping my hand. "Pleased to meetcha. Delighted you joined our team. What's the T.D. stand for?"

"It's a family secret," I said.

"You're kidding."

"I'm kidding. I'm also impressed, Mr. King. Are all these people partners in King-Ducat Salvors?"

He grinned. The gold tooth glinted. "Potentially, my boy," he said, doing a pretty fair impression of W. C. Fields as he waggled an invisible cigar. *"Po-tentially."*

Right about then Kate Starling made her entrance. Dressed in an elegant sky-blue blazer, raw silk blouse, pleated white skirt, and carrying a kid leather portfolio, she looked very much of the class being entertained. Preppy in an unaffected way. Confident, relaxed, all business.

A finger poked me in the small of the back. Mindy whispered, "If you think she looks good now, wait till she makes her pitch. The lady has it down. Boy, *does* she."

Both Harper King and Billy Briggs drifted toward the lady in question. King got there first and nuzzled her cheek briefly. Briggs slipped behind the couple and busied himself opening a panel in the bulkhead. The panel concealed a big-screen television monitor. Briggs inserted a cassette into a video deck.

Kate Starling said, "Everyone have enough bubbly? Lobster tails holding out? Oysters fresh? Fine.

Now, if you'll direct your attention to the screen, we're going to run the video I mentioned. Some of you have seen it before—please bear with us. Running time is a mere fifteen minutes, then both Harp and I will be available to answer any questions you may have."

Jimmy Buffet was cut off in midverse. The conversation settled down to a polite murmur. I helped myself to a plate of goodies and found a seat beside a slender, sixtyish woman whose smile revealed a lot of very expensive dentalwork. On her left hand was a pearl that wasn't quite as big as the oyster on her plate.

Indicating the luxurious surroundings, she said, "Isn't this a gas?"

Fix your wagon, isn't it a gas. *Ducat* was attracting expressions I hadn't heard in years. Someone squeezed my elbow. Mindy, grinning from a row of chairs directly behind me. I grinned back, aware of the dijonnaise sauce on my lips. My new buddy Mindy was a hands-on type. Didn't mean a thing, even if she had instinctively gone for the sweet spot on my elbow.

The video sales pitch was a professional piece of work. Titled *King-Ducat Salvors: The Great Adventure*, it began with computer-generated graphics of the navigable waters in the Straits of Florida. Animated depictions of Spanish trading routes were quickly intercut with shots of antique gold items recovered from famous wrecks. The white-haired woman beside me sighed, as if soothed by the sight of abundant gold.

The next sequence showed Kate Starling at a computer terminal, entering data secured from seventeenth-century shipping manifests, mercantile inventories, and similar documents culled from the Archive of the Indies, the great repository of Spanish shipping records. Turning to the camera, she explained that crucial new evidence, combined with drift, current, and storm data, would enable them to predict the location of a particular wreck. Of which more, it was implied, later. The high-tech stuff segued to long panning shots of *Ducat* under way—taken, obviously, from a helicopter. As the chopper rose, you could see the long curving wake of the little ship, heading bravely out in search of treasure.

Kate Starling handled the voice-over, summarizing the history of Spanish shipping in the Caribbean: the ceaseless royal demands for New World gold to finance Old World wars; the establishment of a primary trade route veering between the Marquesas and the north shores of Cuba; the sources of Archive documentation for an estimated ninety gold-bearing vessels wrecked or lost between 1550 and 1630.

"The dollar value of the lost cargo," she explained, "has been variously estimated at five hundred million to two billion dollars, of which less than three hundred million has been recovered, most of that in the last few years, using modern methods of detection and recovery."

A series of photocopies appeared on the screen. Archive documentation of the galleons *Rosario, San Mateo,* and the pinnace *San Felipe.* We learned that the three ships had departed Veracruz in company of June 17, 1928, bound for Cádiz. Three weeks later the *San Felipe* limped into Nassau and reported that it had lost touch with the two galleons on the night of July 2, when all three vessels had been driven off course by violent and unseasonal winds. It was believed the galleons, being of deeper draft, had struck reef in the Straits of Florida and sunk, presumably with all hands aboard. Lost with them were more than five hundred gold bars, a quantity of coin and silver bar, and a solid-gold crucifix that the governor of Mexico was presenting to the royal court of Spain, as evidence of skilled colonial artisans.

"That the two galleons were loaded with riches beyond imagining is a fact," Kate said. "That they were wrecked in the waters of the Lower Keys is a fact. That the treasure has never been recovered is a fact. What I'm stressing here is that the modern search for this treasure may be an adventure, but it is also a business dealing in facts. Another fact is that like most business, a treasure-salvage operation requires periodic infusions of working capital."

As the voice-over continued, there were shots of Harper King manning *Ducat*'s helm. Ms. Starling described how wooden ships rapidly decayed in the warm waters, leaving little behind but fragile coral formations and deposits of magnetite ballast stones. King grinned into the camera, showing off the gold tooth and pretending to check the magnetometer, a device that was supposed to detect the presence of the old ballast stones. When the magnetometer alarm went off King made a thumbs-up. The sequence looked a little stagy but no one seemed to mind, least of all the affable Captain King, who on cassette appeared to be having a great time starring in his own personal adventure movie.

We saw more of Harper King as he helped Billy Briggs don his diving gear. Briggs did a showboat backflip over the rail—definitely a no-no in the instruction manuals. Then we watched Harp fretting, telling the cameraman that by his calculations his divemaster was out of air. Moments later the camera wobbled, steadying on the water as Briggs broke the surface, waving a mesh bag. The next shot was a topside closeup of an excited—genuinely so, it appeared—Billy Briggs spilling out a few dozen muddy coins. Both he and Harp were talking so fast they sounded like they were on a cocaine jag.

"Now hold on there!" Harp said, speaking live. He shut off the tape deck and held up a chamois leather bag. "Okay folks, enough of the TV talk. If you want to know what makes this whole venture so exciting, it's what I've got in this little purse. First items we recovered, or I should say our divemaster recovered."

Kate Starling, meanwhile, had unrolled a length of dark-green felt. Harp spilled the bag. The doubloons, seemingly untouched by the centuries, were polished to a rich gleam. The lady with the massive pearl slipped by me on the way to the table. Bargain-hunter moves, refined over the decades.

"Hope you appreciate the dramatic touch," Harp said. "This is all we have to show for it so far, and I wanted the 'find' to make an impression. Like Billy and I were impressed when we rinsed off the mud and saw that first glint of yellow."

Briggs had shied away when Kate unfurled the felt—taking a cue, maybe, or perhaps he was genuinely skittish of the limelight. He and Mindy were getting drinks at the bar, taking advantage of the lull. A blender whirred briefly, killed by a signal from Kate Starling, and I saw Mindy stick out her tongue.

"Thirty-two doubloons," Harp was saying. "Estimated value, somewhere between ninety and a hundred and fifty thousand, depending on fluctuations in the rare-coin market. A drop in the bucket, given the operating costs of an expedition like this. An infinitesimally small drop if you consider the documented treasure lost in the *Rosario* expedition exceeds three hundred million dollars—that's just from the manifest. Doesn't take into account any booty or personal effects the captains were intending to smuggle back home."

He went on to explain that although they'd found

a comparatively few doubloons, they hadn't located the precise location of the wreck. Computer simulations of current fluctuations narrowed it down to twelve square miles.

"Which, as any seafaring man will tell you, is one hell of a lot of area. Add that to the fact we can't be sure which galleon the coins spilled from, and you can see we've got our work cut out for us." Harp picked up one of the doubloons and rubbed it thoughtfully in his big hands. "Being a wide-eyed optimist, I'd like to think we found us a few sprinkles from the mother ship *Rosario*, in which case we're talking about five hundred and eight of those sixty-pound gold bars. Anybody got that on the calculator? Works out to a hundred and fifty million in dead-weight value. Not including that solid-gold crucifix. Like I say, I'm a optimist. A pessimist might assume it was only the *San Mateo*, which case we're talking a piddling twenty-six million in loose coin and silver bars."

All the salty talk was giving me a powerful thirst. As I headed for the bar, Harper King was saying, "Is it any wonder we've caught gold fever?"

Mindy followed me to the deck, where we could see the sundowner crowd gathering in Mallory Square. The usual mix of hawkers, gymnasts, and aging flower children, thinned by the derelict season. A few desultory tourists had gathered to watch, more interested in the local characters than the blood-red sky.

I sipped a rum and fresh-squeezed orange juice and asked Mindy if the evening's presentation was typical.

"Well, they always show the same tape. And Harp always stops it like that and brings out the coins. That what you mean?"

I nodded. "The marks the same?"

"The who?"

I cleared my throat, glad she hadn't understood my slip of the tongue. "The investors. Are these birds typical?"

Mindy shrugged. "I guess so. Maybe not always so ritzy, though. Harp says you don't have to be wealthy to invest, not if he keeps the price of the shares down."

It made sense. My experience with the rich was that they were loath to part with even the smallest portion of their money unless the return was guaranteed. Harper King might get lucky with a few high-rollers in the Palm Beach set, but classic confidence schemes depend on ensnaring lots of little people. Like Sammie, with a ten-grand inheritance. And Mindy, working for "shares."

Unless, of course, King-Ducat Salvors was a legitimate operation. I had no way of making that judgment, not yet. Not until I was able to secure more information about the main characters, Harper King and Kate Starling. The mannish boy and the golden girl. Both of them star-quality hustlers.

"Billy says we'll be going out first thing tomorrow," Mindy said. "I can't wait. The longer we're tied up, the more antsy he gets, you know? Clean this, polish that. Not that I mind, really."

I wondered what old Bill was up to. Harp and Kate were still entertaining, trying to close on any potential investors before the champagne wore off. But Briggs was not in the main salon or anywhere on deck. Maybe he'd decided to bunk it early, considering the scheduled predawn start. Somehow I didn't see him as the early-to-bed type.

"I guess Briggs can be tough, huh?"

Mindy shrugged. Plainly she didn't think he was so tough. I wondered if she was aware he had killed a friend who made the mistake of irritating him.

"How'd he happen to get the divemaster position?" I asked.

Mindy gave me a sly look. "Let me guess," she said. "You're after his job, right?"

"Wrong," I said. "No way. I'm in this for kicks—I wouldn't want the responsibility."

On the concrete expanse of the pier, where the performers gathered, two clowns on unicycles were juggling oranges. There was a smattering of applause. Shortly after that a ragged cheer went up as the last hot crescent of the sun slid beneath the horizon. I drained the rum from my glass and leaned on the fine teak rail, feeling reasonably content. A day or two aboard *Ducat* and I would know whether the operation was legit. The luxurious quarters, the lobster tails, the champagne—it was going to be a pleasant way to even the score with Lil Cashman.

Mindy said, "The way I figure, Harp made Billy the divemaster 'cause they been pals for a long time. Used to work at the same job."

I asked her what job that was.

"Billy never said, exactly. What I heard, it was at a country club."

Country clubs. Most people would be put in mind of golf or tennis. When I hear country club I think of an MSF. Better known to civilians as minimum-security facility.

5

I WAS leaning over the rail, gazing at the flock of sailboats moored in the lee of Christmas Tree Island and thinking about turning in, when someone pushed me from behind. It wasn't a real push—there was no danger I'd go over the rail—just a shove meant to get my attention.

"Yo, bubba," Billy said. "Up for a beer or three?"

I unclenched my fists and put on a bashful smile. Pancho to his Cisco Kid. Getting to know Wild Bill was part of the job, like it or not.

"Lead the way," I said.

We walked across the square to Front Street. A cruise ship was in. The tourists were drifting through the streets like gauzy bits of flotsam, murmuring in mysterious tongues. Billy ignored them. I followed him into a cul-de-sac that housed the entrance to the Pirates Den, the last of the Old Town topless clubs. There was a big tattooed biker running the door. He and Briggs went through a complicated, muscular handshake and we took stools at the bar. Like the bouncer, the barmaid seemed to be on intimate terms with Billy.

"Beer and a kick," she said, setting a bottle and a shot of schnapps on the moist counter in front of him. The lacy, Frederiks of Hollywood thing she had on was meant to be noticed. She did a little turn, showing off the merchandise. Not badly formed, but no one outside of a catalogue can truss up in lacy gear like that and not look a little silly.

"You lookin' hot, Estelle," Billy said. Estelle was pleased. Evidently she thought it important to impress Billy Briggs.

It was early in the scheme of things for the Den, which tends toward late-night entertainment of a sort. A kootch dancer padded around the raised stage, snapping her G-string listlessly, out of sync with a disco tune. Hard to work up any enthusiasm when only a handful of young and deeply embarrassed Coast Guard seamen had taken seats at crotch level.

"Look at those farmers," Billy said. "I bet they never been laid."

I found it was possible to drink from a bottle of beer without letting the rim touch my lips. One of the recruits, egged on by his pals, had worked up the courage to try slipping a dollar bill into the kootch dancer's G-string. Encouraged, she put a little more action into her hips.

Billy chugged his first beer. A second appeared on the bar before he was done, with another schnapps chaser in a little plastic cup.

"Stash," he said, stifling a burp, "how'd you get a name like that?"

"My father's name was Staskowski."

"And he shortened it up?"

"My mother did," I said. "After he died. For sentimental reasons. Stash was his nickname."

"Whatever you say. Hey," he said, hooking a finger on a piece of lace as Estelle went by, "when's Cindy Ann on?"

"She's next," the barmaid said, slipping adroitly out his grasp. "There's only the two of them this week, so she's always next."

Billy nodded. "Cindy Ann is hot," he confided.

"Call herself Candy. This one on now, she's Taffy. She don't really dance much, not like Cindy Ann."

A tourist couple came in the door, took one look at what was happening on stage, and quickly backed out, like crawfish scuttling into a hiding place in the reef.

"So, Bill," I said, "how'd you and Harper King happen to cross paths?"

Briggs scuffed his knuckles through his crew cut. The way the bar lights were aimed it was hard to get a fix on his small gray eyes. "I guess what he did," he said uneasily. "He asked around. You know, at the dive shops, like that. Wanted him a local diver, somebody knows the waters."

"You think we'll find it? The motherlode?"

He shrugged. "We got a shot, I guess." Downing the schnapps seemed to give him confidence. "You getting in on the ground floor, bubba. We hit the jackpot, we *all* of us get rich."

"King must already be rich, huh? With a boat like that?"

"I guess so. Hell, he must be, you're right." Clearly it was a subject that needed changing. "Better drink up," he advised. "Weather holds, we may be out there for a couple days."

At first I made a show of keeping up with him. Soon enough he lost interest in what I was or wasn't drinking. He was inhaling schnapps so fast his breath smelled like something vented from a peppermint factory. It suited me that Billy get drunk. Not that he needed any encouragement.

"Come on, you sea farmers!" he roared at the young Coast Guard recruits. "What ever happened to *Semper Paratus?*" He turned to me and muttered, "Helpless little fuckers. Have to show 'em how."

Hitching up his belt, Briggs swaggered to the stage. Grinning ferociously, he clamped a dollar bill in his teeth and beckoned to Taffy. She obliged by placing her hands on his shoulders and humping the air just above his chin. When she moved away the money was there in her G-string. The Coast Guard cheered.

"Warmin' 'em up for Cindy Ann," he explained in a husky voice before upending another dose of schnapps. The gray eyes had turned flat and mean. Briggs had passed over to the other side, entered a world all his own. I decided to try prodding him while the communication channels were still partly open.

"So tell me, Billy, what do you really think of the Harp and Kate show?"

"What's that supposed to mean?"

"You know, the presentation. The video thing."

He leaned in close, gassing peppermint in my face. "You got what I call a wise-ass attitude, Stash ol' buddy. Definite wise-ass."

"So I've been told."

" 'Sokay," he said, settling back on the stool. "Why should I care? I ain't gettin' paid to care. I'm gettin' paid to *dive*, understand?"

I said got the idea.

"An' you gettin' paid, shares and a little cash, gettin' paid to do what I say, and what I say is this. Mind your business. Okay?"

"A-OK, Bill. You're the boss. Here, have another on me."

"Decent," he said. "Decent."

"So it must have been a thrill, finding those doubloons, huh?"

"Real thrill."

"Lucky shot, the camera just happens to be there when you come up. Really made that video click."

I almost had him going. Then Cindy Ann came out from the dressing room and Billy Briggs forgot all about me. Candy—that was her stage name—had a long mane of platinum hair that went down to the cleft of her buttocks. I had about decided it was a wig when she did something with it that meant the hair had to be real even if the color came out of a bottle. The barmaid noticed the look on my face.

"That Cindy Ann," she said, grinning, "she got an amazing talent, huh? I said to her, I go, 'Honey, you could be an acrobat, like in the circus.' What it is, she's double jointed."

"At the very least," I said.

Billy moved closer to the stage. He made no attempt to repeat his trick with the dollar bill between his teeth. What he did was stand there was his arms folded, swaying to the thumping music while Cindy Ann went through her remarkable contortions.

"You know what?"

I looked around and found Estelle the barmaid so close her lace blurred.

"What?"

"Don't take this wrong now. All I'm saying, he got that look in his eye, Billy has. Any minute he's gonna get mean. Better have yourself ready to deal with him."

"I appreciate the warning."

"Don't tell him I said nothing. Please?"

I assured her it wouldn't be mentioned. Not that Billy's temper was exactly a state secret. It was as plain as the scowl on his face when he came back to the bar.

"I'm a go over the Chart Room," he announced. "Bust me some heads."

"Have another here," I said, handing him a schnapps. "One for the road."

He swallowed the drink and crushed the plastic cup under his heel. He was on edge, waiting for someone to dare him. I did my level best.

"So, Bill, what's the story with Kate Starling? Some action she's got, huh?"

Something clicked on in his eyes. A warning light. "What's that supposed to mean?"

"Means she walks real nice, Bill. You know? Means she's got movie-star looks. Hell, *you* know what it means."

He backed me against the bar, using his inflated chest and his bad breath. "Look here, wise-ass. Kate and Harp are tight. Real tight. Now don't you forget that. Harp's my *friend*, okay?" He jabbed a blunt forefinger in my solar plexus, hard enough to make me wince. "Harp may look like a big Baby Huey, bubba, but you try to get cute with his woman, he's liable to crack your spine. Or maybe *I* will."

If you're going to get through a bar fight without getting banged up, you have to plan ahead. You need to have an idea of who will do what to whom. The biker at the door was moving in cautiously. It was important that he not think of me as an instigator, once it started. I put my arm around Billy's broad shoulders and made it look like I was trying to calm him down.

Leaning close, I said, "I thought what you did, Billy, was crack beer mugs, not spines."

I could feel it coming, telegraphed by the muscles in his shoulders. I dropped to one knee and the fist burned the air over my head. Not connecting threw Briggs off balance. He staggered, colliding with the biker. That set him off again. This time the swing connected, hitting the biker in the neck. He swore and tried to grab hold of Billy's fists. Big mistake. I didn't see how it happened, but all of a sudden blood was coming out of the biker's nose.

"Get 'em out of here," Estelle said from behind the bar. She had the telephone in her hand, threatening to dial.

"Hey, Billy Boy," I shouted, "yer mother wears army boots!"

I didn't expect him to appreciate the absurdity of schoolboy insults. I expected him to swing and he did. I was backpedaling quicker than an NFL quarterback. His fist scuffed my chin—he was faster than he looked. The booze was throwing his timing off, not his speed.

We spilled through the door into the narrow cul-de-sac. There were vending carts shoved up along the building. I grabbed one and wheeled it around. Billy charged into it. I caught sight of his grin in the light spilling out of the Pirates Den. Billy was having fun. A good, old-fashioned bar brawl was his idea of a good time.

Not that he was capable, at that moment, of forming coherent ideas. He was all energy and muscle and instinct. If he'd wanted to grab hold of me, he might have done so. Instead, he wanted to land a roundhouse punch. That made it relatively simple to avoid getting hit. The key was to watch his fists as he reared back and let it go. The momentum would carry him all the way around, spinning off balance.

Billy had plenty of power. It was the schnapps that made him unfocused, wide of the mark. I felt like a toreador. My chin was the cape he charged at. Every now and then, to vary the game and keep him off balance, I would duck behind a vending cart or swivel it into his path.

Before long we attracted an audience. The biker Billy had popped stood there glowering, holding a paper towel to his nose. Behind him, as if seeking a safe vantage point, was Cindy Ann. She had a leather jacket over her shoulders, borrowed, evidently, from the biker.

"Billy, honey, stop it now, heah?"

If he heard, he didn't heed. I think he was listening only to the urge to connect his fists with a target. Me, as it happened. Foam flecked at his lips. The air

sang, I ducked, he spun. It became a kind of dangerous dance. With his weight and power a solid blow
would shatter bone. I had a long-standing policy
against letting my bones get shattered.

"Billy, honey, *please!*"

I had to keep my concentration on the balled fists,
the way his feet pointed, telegraphing his next move.
The biker and Cindy Ann, flanked by a few of the
Coast Guard recruits, were aspects of my peripheral
vision. To be reckoned into the overall picture. I caught
a glimpse of the biker's eyes. He wasn't happy about
getting his nose busted. Not even a little bit. No
sense of humor.

"*Bill-eee!*"

Cindy Ann had a lovely figure, pretty hair. Her
voice left a lot to be desired. A girl in my sixth-grade
civics class had a similar whine and then as now it
set my teeth on edge.

"Chuck-ee, *do* something. He's gonna get hurt."

Chucky was the biker. He wanted to do something, all right. Unlike Cindy Ann, he wasn't interested in saving Billy's ass. Not that I wanted Billy's
ass, or any part of him. It would have been simple
enough to duck under one of his wild missiles and
drive a fist upward, into the tender spot under his
ribs. The problem was, Billy would remember a blow
like that and I needed to have him on my side, come
the morning.

I decided to let Chucky do the necessary. Feinting
right, I dived left and came up on my feet. Billy
spun all the way around, staggering. I ducked again
and led him back toward the door, toward good old
Chuck. The sight of his biker pal with the clotted
paper towel on his nose distracted Billy. He forgot
me for just a moment and focused on the towel and
the blood. Then he made his mistake. He laughed.

Hee hee hee.

It came out like a donkey wheeze because by then Billy was starting to lose his wind. The biker didn't bother raising his fists. He merely flung his boot out and landed a solid blow between Billy's legs.

"Oh, Bill-eeeee!"

Billy didn't respond to Cindy's Ann's whine. He was too busy going down. His eyes went white, he sighed, and then he toppled, like one of those buildings they dynamite from the basement. Collapsing inward in slow motion. As his knees hit the pavement his hands cupped his genitals. Chucky had his boot cocked, ready to connect with Billy's unguarded face.

"Oops," I said, catching the boot.

Chuck shook me off. "Fucking bastard," he said. I think he meant Billy. But the boot stayed down. It was an instinct, that attempt at a killing blow, and he didn't try to repeat it.

Cindy Ann was on her knees. She had Billy's head cradled in her lap. He was out cold, the semblance of a smile twisted his foam-flecked lips.

"You big dummy," she said, "doncha ever learn?"

6

IN THE dream I was in my hammock, listening to storm waters flood over the island. Wavelets splashed against the porch. The ficus tree loomed in the shadows, rustling wet leaves. There was something comforting about the quiet gurgle of the rising flood; I was safe as long as I stayed in the hammock, in the dream.

I woke up to find *Ducat* under way. The sea roiled against the aluminum hull, not six inches from my head. In some part of my sleeping mind I'd been aware of that since the big diesels first began to surge. Moving at medium throttle through large, uncrested swells from the sound of it—ripples left behind when the hurricane died.

I lay in the bunk, enjoying the sensation of being again at sea, until someone's knuckles rapped against the teak door. The guest cabin they'd assigned me was one of three on the portside, opposite the engine room. I unlatched the door and found Mindy in her bathrobe, eyes squinting with sleep.

" 'Morning," I said, putting more cheer into it than I felt.

Mindy blinked, bracing herself as the deck canted. "Three-thirty," she muttered thickly. "This is supposed to be Billy's job, the wake-up call. Anyhow, coffee on the bridge, you want it."

I dressed and went topside. There was, indeed,

good strong coffee available on the bridge, and reasonably fresh croissants as well. No weevily ship's biscuit for *Ducat*'s crew, no sirree. First class all the way. I poured a mug of the coffee and checked out the electronic goodies. As the dish mounted on the antenna mast had indicated, the vessel was equipped with the latest in satellite navigational systems. Backup for the Sat-Nav was a powerful Loran unit. The high-tech toys included color radar, side-scanning sonar, ship-to-shore radio gear, and the magnetometer featured in the video presentation. All very state-of-the-art and professional. If there was a scam, it didn't involve shortcuts in the necessary equipment.

Beyond the bow the seas were dark, almost indistinguishable from the starless sky. Harper King had the helm on autopilot. He was nibbling on a croissant and watching the radar screen.

"Black as pitch out there," he said, his voice soft. "I'm sitting here letting the boat steer itself, and you know what I'm thinking? I'm thinking about those old-timers, the ones used to navigate by the seat of their pants. Compass and dead reckoning, shot of the stars if they were lucky. My God! No *wonder* they run so many ships up on the damned reef."

The autohelm started to beep. Instinctively I moved toward the wheel.

"Wait," Harp said. "Give it a chance."

There was a whirring noise in the pedestal. I felt the hull shift and turn onto a new heading.

Behind me Harp chuckled. "Amazing, huh?" he said. "You line her up on the first buoy out of the harbor, they program the course. Self-correcting all the way."

"But you keep a watch."

"Absolutely," he said. "I got a radar warning signal tied into the program, supposed to set off an alarm if we approach another vessel on an opposing course. But I only trust this computer stuff so far. So the helm is always manned. Rule number one."

"Number two?"

"The coffeepot is always full. Very important. Only drug we keep on board is caffeine—that's related to rule number three: no drugs. You may have heard we've been boarded a couple of times already. So if you've got anything, even a little reefer, get rid of it, okay?"

"Only thing I've smoked lately is a little wahoo."

"What's that?" he asked, looking surprised. "Like Maui Wowee?"

"More like a fish. They run about ten, fifteen pounds. Tasty any way you care to cook them. Me, I put the fillets in a smoker, use the hardwood briquets. Smoked wahoo, slice of Bermuda onion, little chilled vodka. That's my idea of a perfect high."

Harp laughed until tears came to his eyes. Flecks of croissant stuck to his lips. He brushed them away with the back of his hand. "You had me going there," he said when he'd got his breath back. "We're going to get along fine. No question."

I asked where Billy Briggs was.

"Sent him to bed," Harp said. "He showed up here just when I was getting ready to cast off, stinking of booze. Looked like he got into a fight. Situation like that, best thing is to let him sleep it off."

"You want me to take a watch?"

"Nah. Just stick around, shoot the breeze," he said, squinting toward the bow, where the shapeless dark was in transit, gradually getting lighter. "Gets kind of spooky up here. Hour of the wolf, know what I mean?"

Harp King and I watched night drain from the sky, the black sea transformed into the silver mirror shards of dawn. He tossed his coffee down like a dipso dropping shots of rotgut and asked what I knew about the territorial instincts of sharks.

"Reason I ask, last time out I had this little incident with a hammerhead," he said. "Big mother, maybe fifteen feet. We were swimming patterns close to the bottom, Billy and me and Kate. Mindy had the topside watch. What happens, the hammer circles around—I'm trying to stay cool, just watching—next thing it suddenly charges in, tries to take a bite out of my scuba tank."

"Ouch."

"First thing I did was piss my trunks," Harp said, staring into the empty coffeecup. "Then I must have hit the cartridge on the BC vest because I went straight up forty feet like I was launched from a rocket. Mindy got in the water and took me back down."

The way he said "took me back down" sent a little shiver through me. Implied was the need for immediate recompression to avoid an embolism—those deadly bubbles of air that may pass into a diver's bloodstream if he ascends too fast without continually exhaling. Dive manuals will tell you never to recompress a panicked diver by taking him back down. The idea is, you pack up immediately and get the victim to a recompression tank as quickly as possible. That's in dive manuals. In the real world recompression tanks are often too far away—an embolism can kill or paralyze in minutes—and sometimes the only recourse is to head back down.

In Harp's case the gamble had paid off. Forty feet of depth was about maximum for the kind of hurried ascent he described. Had he been twenty feet deeper, his chances of surfacing unscathed would have been about the same as hitting the Trifecta at Hialeah.

"You're familiar with these waters," he said. "Ever

seen the same shark hanging around the same piece
of real estate?''

"Only at the condominiums," I said. "Usually
they're wearing polyester suits and drinking marga-
ritas. Seriously, it's a great big ocean. Chances are
you'll never see that particular shark again."

"That's what Billy tells me," he said, sounding
unconvinced.

"Whatever you do, don't go back down if you feel
anxious about it," I said. "Macho divers get to be
dead divers, sooner or later."

"What I'm thinking," he said. "I got me one of
those bang sticks. You know, a shark killer. I figure
a twelve-gauge shotgun slug ought to take care of a
hammerhead."

I agreed it would. I'd never liked the idea of bang
sticks—firearms are dangerous enough abovewater—
but then I'd never had a shark try to eat my air tank.
If the bang stick made him feel secure, fine. I decided then and there never to sneak up behind Harper
King while he was underwater. Or above it, for that
matter.

We dropped anchor about forty miles southwest
of Key West. The early-morning sky was burnt-orange
where it blurred into the undulating horizon. According to the depth readout we were in thirty-eight
feet of water, over a sandy bottom. Harp made a
point of clearing the Sat-Nav screen of the coordinates before I could steal a look. Exact location would
be divulged on a need-to-know basis—he hoped I
wouldn't be offended.

"We make a find, everyone on the crew will get
the numbers," he said, sounding apologetic. "For
now I'd just as soon keep my little secrets."

That made two of us.

I was up in the bow, making the sure the anchor

chain had enough slack to absorb the steady rise and fall of the swells, when Kate and Mindy came on deck. A sexy Mutt and Jeff pair: the tall, lithe blonde and the petite, dark-haired beauty. Not your typical tattooed salvage divers, by any means.

Kate came right to the point. "Mindy tells me you're a fishing guide. I told Billy to sign up an experienced local *diver*, not a local *guide*. No offense."

"This week I'm a two-for-one special."

"Meaning?"

"Meaning," I said, grinning right into her designer shades, "you're welcome to check my references. I run a guide boat when the tarpon are biting, like Mindy told you. Other times I do other things. Like diving. I'm certified on scuba, hard hat, and hookah."

Kate Starling lifted up her shades and studied me. Behind her Mindy was making faces, trying to signal a message to me—what, I didn't know.

"Okay," Kate said, dropping the shades. "Just checking. I thought maybe you were one of Billy's barroom cronies, along for the ride."

She gave me a big smile that was supposed to make me feel all better, and headed for the rear deck.

Mindy was blushing under her tan. "We were just chatting," she said. "You know, making small talk? I never meant her to think . . . Are you really pissed at me, Stash?"

"Has Billy hired any of his drinking buddies?"

She thought about it. "Well, there was this one dude," she said, "he never even suited up. Said he was having an allergic reaction, clogged up his sinuses. Harp had to let him go."

"Then I guess Miss Starling has a right to be concerned."

Mindy gave me a quick, sexless hug. I responded, aware of the firmness of her shoulders, the strength in her compact frame. "Boy," she said. "You ought to see the flinty look you get. It's kind of scary."

"Must be your imagination."

"Uh uh," she said. "I don't think so. For a second there I felt like you thought I was just some jerk kid trying to ruin your day. It wasn't a nice feeling."

The fist in my stomach unclenched. Maybe Kate Starling really was concerned about my credentials. Or maybe she just didn't want any outsiders sniffing around the salvage operation. Whatever, it was a sure thing Kate Starling wouldn't be having any problem with feisty hammerheads. She was a match for any shark, finned or two-legged.

"Penny for your thoughts," Mindy said. "I might even spring for a dime."

"Save your money," I said. "I was thinking I'd like another cup of coffee. Care to join me?"

But what nagged was the uneasy feeling that life aboard *Ducat* wasn't going to be the laid-back romp I'd expected. If the operation was scam, uncovering it was going to be a tough as, well, finding gold at the bottom of the sea.

7

B ILLY BRIGGS, divemaster, came out from under his rock an hour or so after we anchored. By then Mindy and I had the gear laid out on the teak grid of the dive platform and were lounging in the shade under the awning, awaiting instruction. The swells had moderated. The wind was a steady five knots, as warm as breath. From where I sat the outriggers on a fleet of shrimpers were just barely visible, marching south into the Gulf.

Briggs was wearing black nylon briefs, a pair of rubber thongs, and Ray-Bans to hide his bloodshot eyes. He walked with a slight limp. His sun-bleached crew cut was matted and bristly, like the knap of an unkempt rug.

"Get me an egg," he told Mindy.

Without a word she jumped up and made for the galley. I got the impression she was familiar with Billy's morning-after routine. He hawked and spat over the side, then snapped the waist of the briefs, adjusting himself. "Fucking Pirate's Den," he said. "Guy runs the door over there, he had it in for me last night. Kicked me in the balls for no reason."

If Billy had chosen to forget certain crucial events, I saw no reason to remind him. Mindy returned with a whole egg and a mug of heavily creamed coffee. Briggs tipped back his head, expertly cracked the egg over his open mouth, and swallowed it raw. What a guy.

After he finished the coffee he sighed, adjusted the pouch of his briefs again, and said, "Okay, I'm human. Let's get the boss and the boss lady down here, we'll go over the chart."

Harp came down the ladder from the bridge, a chart tube clenched under his arm. Boss lady followed. She had put on a bright-green bikini that covered the essentials, no more. Such minuscule attire is not exactly rare in my part of the world, but I had to make an effort not to gawk. Bad form to openly lust for another man's mate, although Harper King had the cocky grin of a mind reader.

"Here it is, me hearties," he said, knocking the chart from the tube and spreading it out on the table under the awning. "Bluebeard's sunken treasure, the lost gold of the Incas, remains of the Spanish galleon *Rosario*, take your pick."

It was a computer printout, ruled off in quadrants. King used the blunt end of a pencil as a pointer. "Ballast stones," he said. "You can see how they start down here, just a few, then fill in pretty heavy. Sprayed out over three hundred yards, more or less. They're pretty well encrusted, but we had samples lab-tested and the stones are definitely magnetite, which means Spanish origin. Probably prior to 1800, from the shape and the iron content. Ballast dropped on a sandy bottom about a mile this side of the reef. Like she tore herself open and made it this far before coming apart. Billy found the coins over in this quadrant." He pointed to a square marked with a red X, about ninety feet from the main ballast deposit. "We've already worked a square of quadrants around the coin location. Nothing. My thinking is some poor bastard went over the side with his pocket full. All the coins were found inside a three-foot radius, which is consistent with coming out of a small purse. Just a theory. We'll continue to survey quadrants in that area, of course, but my gut instinct is, we have to go for the cannon."

He paused, rubbing the pencil thoughtfully in the cleft of his chin. The lecture was for my benefit and he wanted to make sure I was following.

"Cannon?" I asked dutifully.

"Each galleon carried twenty-four bronze cannon, twelve to a side. Some may have broken loose, but chances are most of the armament went down with the hull. With this kind of bottom they could be under as much as four feet of silt. Unless," he said, pausing for effect, "this little blow we had uncovered the sons of bitches for us. Now wouldn't *that* be sweet," he said to Briggs.

"Pretty deep to get stirred up much," Billy said. "We'll know when we go down. Maybe the bottom current raised something."

Harp elected himself tender, which meant he would be keeping the topside watch. Whistling cheerfully, he set up a dive clock, a ledger, and a portable weather radio. Copies of the Navy Emergency Decompression Tables were encased in plastic sleeves and weighted down under a conch shell. Spare tanks were stacked under the davit, ready to be dropped over the side when needed. A triple hookah rig was set up with a compressor, the hoses neatly coiled, should it be required.

Harp snapped on a plastic sun visor emblazoned with a King-Ducat Salvors logo and settled into a deck chair.

"Find me something shiny," he said.

Briggs, meanwhile, had made a miraculous recovery. After clearing his eyes with Murine and his sinuses with nasal spray, he handed his gear over the transom and executed a one-hand vault to the platform, demonstrating his upper-body strength. Not bad for a guy who'd had, at most, four hours' sleep.

"The weighted buoys in the net bag are to mark out quadrants," he said. "I'll show you the routine when we get down to the site. The yellow flags we'll use to mark any spot we get a positive reading. These new detectors are supposed to pick up concentrations of base metal, like bronze or silver or gold. The needle dial is a little hard to read, but you'll get the hang of it."

My black neoprene dive suit was hot to the touch. I powdered down with talc, but it didn't help much. Mindy and Kate were suited up while I was still struggling into my pants. By the time I had the BC vest on and the weight belt cinched I was swimming in perspiration. The two women were already in the water, vests inflated while they waited for the slower menfolk.

I could feel Billy Briggs watching me. Checking out my form like a good divemaster. I sat on the edge of the platform, legs in the water, and slipped the double-tank harness over my shoulders. He tapped me on the top of my head.

"What's wrong with this picture?" Billy said quietly.

I looked down at my waist. "Damn," I said, embarrassed. "My weights."

I'd put the tank harness on over the weight belt, making it impossible to shed instantly, in the event of an emergency. A definite no-no. I slid the harness back and tried again. Billy nodded approval. "No sweat, bubba," he said. "What say you buddy up with me, for the first dive?"

"Good deal," I said, pulling my mask into place, making sure it was sealed. I hooked the carry loop of the metal detector to my belt and slipped into the water.

Harp King, using the boat hoist, had set a heavily moored dive buoy off the stern. I made for it, loosening a vent in my wet suit. Relatively cool water jetted in, providing quick relief. At the buoy I put the mouthpiece in, checked the air pressure. Satisfied that the regulator was functioning, I bled my BC vest and dropped, fins first.

When the storm of bubbles cleared, the first thing I saw was the bright orange of Mindy's wet suit. She grinned around her mouthpiece and made an okay sign.

Welcome to the wet world, man-thing.

Below, two pairs of translucent yellow power fins flashed as Kate and Billy pirouetted slowly around the buoy line. A *pas de deux* through pillars of light, spiraling downward. Mindy followed, hands trailing at her hips, venting a stream of silver bubbles.

I cleared the last reserves from my buoyancy vest and let the weights carry me down, conserving air. Determined not to gobble the stuff like an excited amateur. Responding, despite my better judgment, to the machismo standard set by Billy Briggs. Or was it Kate Starling?

I drifted down through a school of yellow jacks. They shimmered, keeping their distance, effortlessly readjusting at precise intervals. Skittish things, they had probably been disturbed from their feeding pattern when the buoy line was dropped. Seen from my guide boat, the jacks would have been targets of opportunity, candidates for the fry pan. But upon entering their world I tend to think of fish, no matter how delectable, as fellow inhabitants—they simply cease to look like food. A sentiment spearfisherpersons don't share.

Billy was waiting on the sandy bottom, reclining with his chin in his hand, showing off. He looked like a vulcanized Chesire cat. Kate Starling was adjusting her BC vest, finding neutral buoyancy. Mindy, exuberant, tucked her knees up and executed a slow roll. I had to clear my mask and managed it with a minimum of fuss, blinking the sting of saltwater from my eyes. High overhead the bottomside of *Ducat* penetrated the rippling mirror of the surface like a fat thumb stuck through Jell-O.

Reminded of Harp's tale of an encounter with a feisty hammerhead, I looked around. No sign of shark, or any other large forbidding shapes within the forty-foot radius of visibility at the bottom.

Billy used a hand-held directional finder to home in on a submersible radio beacon that had been secured at the site. The alternative would have been to fix a permanent surface buoy—certain to attract claim jumpers or other curious interlopers. We swam for less than a minute before spotting the first yellow quadrant markers floating a foot or so above the bottom. Billy altered course slightly, riding over the row of markers, heading for the scattered ballast stones that marked the site of the wreck.

The bottom dipped slightly. A school of parrotfish came briefly into view, darting away as Billy kicked forward. I saw coral-encrusted stones rising out of the sand. The gully on the opposite side was probably caused by the pile of ballast interfering with the flow of the bottom current. As is always the case with coral formations, life teemed nearby. It made me wish we were night diving, when the colors would be bright and true in artificial light. At this depth, in daytime, the visible palette was limited to grayish greens and pale yellows. Through the faceplate it looked like someone had tweaked the color adjustment out of whack.

With our "base" established, Billy Briggs set us to work. The quadrants to be explored had been set out on a north-south-east-west grid. Each quadrant was about twenty feet on a side. The idea was to run the metal detector slowly over every single inch of each quadrant, using a weighted, inflatable buoy to mark any positive reading. That's when the romance of treasure hunting started to wear off. The current wasn't particularly strong, but just keeping your place tended to erode your strength after a while. The bottom had a sameness to it that became bleak.

Billy worked a set of quadrants nearby, keeping an eye on his newest diver. Beyond him I could barely make out Mindy's athletic form. Kate, I knew, was staking out more quadrants on the other side of the ballast deposit. My own metal detector seemed so stubbornly unresponsive I kept checking the power grid, just be sure it was functioning.

I never had cause to drop a marker buoy that first day. My quadrants were as barren as moon dust. I became a robot, swimming in precise formation, conserving my energy, totally absorbed with watching the unresponsive meter on the detector.

The tedium was broken once, when a big manta ray passed between me and the bottom, a gap of less than two feet. Gliding like some futuristic flying wing, it rippled effortlessly over the sand in awesome, thunderous silence. Three hundred pounds if it was an ounce. After it veered away into the mists I thumped my chest to make sure my heart was still functioning and caught Billy Briggs grinning at me. From his angle he'd probably seen the ray sweeping toward me. I waved—ha ha, Bill, didn't scare me a bit.

We stayed at the bottom for two double-tank changes, about the maximum working time for the depth. Even the warmest Gulf waters will erode body temperatures after a few hours. As the newest one on the team, I got tapped as the first to ascend. I hooked the useless detector on my belt and went up, keeping pace with my exhaust bubbles.

Harp King was waiting on the dive platform, ready to take my gear.

"What's it like down there?" he wanted to know.

When I got my breath back I said, "Probably the movie will be more exciting. They'll edit out the dull parts."

"See my buddy down there?"

I had to think about what he meant. "No," I said. "Mr. Hammerhead was not in attendance. Mr. Manta Ray was, though. Spooked hell out of me."

"You didn't hit your inflator, though."

True enough. The encounter with the big ray had been more of a thrill, not a panic of fear. Which had a lot to do with the fact that a manta ray, though large and alien, is not a predator. I said as much to Harp, but he shrugged it off. He didn't want anyone making excuses for him.

"Tending was what I wanted to do today," he said. "Tomorrow, or whenever, I'm going back down."

"Whatever you want," I said. "Don't force it."

"Hey, there's gold in that there mud," he said, mimicking a Hollywood-style western drawl. "I just feel lucky, is all."

I stripped off the wet suit and was suddenly hit by the aftereffects of the dive. My knees were weak. My muscles felt like I'd been handling a jackhammer all day. The hot August sun failed to warm my innards. I left Harp crouched on the platform, waiting for the next diver up, and went below for a change of clothes.

Billy's cabin was two doors from mine. I tried the handle, more out of nosy habit than real curiosity. Locked, and no surprise. If Billy had learned anything after two years in Raiford, it was the value of privacy. Besides, I wasn't sure I wanted or needed to know what a guy like Billy would hide under his mattress.

In my cabin I stripped, got into the shower stall,

and tested the *Ducat*'s supply of hot water. More
than adequate. Ten minutes at near scalding and I
felt human again, warm at the core. The knees were
still a bit weak, but it would take me a few days to
get back into prime diving shape.

On the way up to the main deck I made a detour
to the bridge, confident that Harp would be occu-
pied with getting his other divers aboard. The first
thing I did was pour a mug of coffee. That was for
cover. Then, whistling casually, I sidled over to the
navigator's station and switched on the Sat-Nav unit.
The series of digits displayed on the screen meant
nothing to me, but I memorized them for future
reference. The exact location of the claim site might
be useful information.

I heard bare feet padding up the companionway at
about the time I turned off the screen. When Kate
Starling entered the bridge I was at the coffee machine, opening a packet of sugar.

"Find anything interesting?" she said.

I held up the mug of coffee and made shivering
motions. Kate was still in her micro-bikini, more or
less, and her skin was pocked with goose bumps
from the inner cold of the dive. She was shivering
and her right fist was clenched, her knuckles showing white.

"I didn't mean up here," she said, her eyes flicking to the dark screen of the Sat-Nav. "I meant at
the site."

I nodded, pretending I'd understood all along.
"So far, just a lot of sand. Any luck with you?"

She nodded, her teeth chattering. Then she opened
her hand and I saw the unmistakable glint of gold.

8

"S HE CAME up with this gorgeous little gold bracelet," I told Lily Cashman over sundowners at the Laughing Gull. "Harp says from the markings and the quality it must have been crafted by the Dutch artisans the Spaniards brought to the New World. I'll have to take his word for it. All I know is, it's a thing of beauty."

You can always tell when Lil is skeptical. Her green eyes hood like a lizard's and the point of her tongue makes a pink punctuation in the corner of her mouth. Maybe it's a trick she learned in law school, but it worked well enough to make me doubt everything I'd been telling her for the last twenty minutes.

"Sounds expensive," Lil murmured, stirring her cocktail with a celery stalk. "Maybe they bought it with Sammie's ten grand."

We were out on the dock at the tiki bar, under the palm-frond roof. Lil had ordered a serving of conch fritters but didn't seem to mind me helping her clean the plate. The late lunch I'd had as *Ducat* returned to port hadn't touched the hollow in my belly. A day working at forty feet will burn off a whole lot of calories. Hard-hat divers, the boys working the oil rigs, eat like lumberjacks.

Hunger momentarily abated, I leaned back in my chair and tried to mimic Lil's lizard look. Hooding my eyes just made it hard to see. She noticed and poked me in the ankle. "Very funny, T.D. Now cut it out and tell me how I'm going to get Sam's money back."

"You might try asking."

Lil snorted. I decided she wasn't a lizard, she was a pretty version of a Komodo dragon. "Give me some credit," she said. "I wouldn't have asked for your help if I hadn't already struck out. First thing I do, when Sammie finally tells me, is I pick up the phone and check with the A.G.'s office, determine the current status of King-Ducat ink, and this dubious share offering. I get good news and bad news. The good news is the corporation is registered, which means they probably intend to abide by the strictures of the securities regulations. The bad news is the law says any company making a time-share offering—and that's how the King-Ducat shares are classified, odd as it may seem—has to give investors forty-eight hours to change their minds. That's bad because Sammie didn't work up the courage to tell me what she'd done with the money until a week after Harper King and that ice-blond honey of his cashed her check. What happened, Sammie got taken in by that dog and pony show. You know, the champagne, the slick video presentation, the grand finale with the gold coins."

"It's very persuasive."

The dragon finished her drink and sighed. It was a large sigh, big enough to embrace the idea of a credulous male who was, in her opinion, solid bone from ear to ear. "T.D., do me a favor. Wipe that dumbstruck look off your face. And if it means you're falling for that long-legged sociopath who's managing the money for Harper King, I'll hire someone to feed you to the alligators."

"You're jealous," I said, grinning.

"Uh huh, no way. I just know a nickel-plated bitch when I see one. What happened, I went down there to that sleazy, overrigged boat they've got and I explained to Miss Starling how I was representing a client who had mistakenly invested every penny she had in the world in an extremely risky enterprise and that any subsequent legal action might be avoided if Miss Starling would just buy the four shares back. I say, 'No hard feelings, we'll just call it an error in judgment.' Little Miss Legs gives me this very cool smile and says, 'No hard feelings, honey, but a deal is a deal.' "

"And that's when you came to me."

"The woman is bad news. I can feel it in my bones."

The evening sky had the ephemeral look of a hand-tinted photograph. I got another beer from the bar and made a detour to the jukebox on the way back to the table. Leon Russell, with that southern fatback voice of his. I lip-synched the first verse to Lil. She didn't appreciate my mugging, so I coaxed her out of her chair and waltzed her along the dock while old Leon crooned about searching and not finding and being lost, lost in a masquerade.

When the song was over the dragon look was gone. "I'm being just a little bit bitchy," Lil said. "Just a teensy weeny. Sorry."

"Never mind about that. What you're supposed to say is, 'Gosh, T.D., I never dreamed you danced like Fred Astaire.' "

"More like Ginger Rogers."

"Take that back."

"You'll be careful, won't you? I'm not kidding about this bad feeling."

"Relax," I said. "We're going to have fun now."

Mutt has a habit of sleeping with his eyes open.

There is something disconcerting about a man looking at you while he's snoring. I propped his straw hat over his face and went about my business. After a while the snoring stopped and his growly voice came from under the hat, demanding to know who the hell was breaking into his shack.

"Door was open, Mutt. Door is always open."

He sat up, rubbing a hand over his brown, egg-bald head. "What's this I hear about you hired on the *Loveboat*?"

"*Ducat.*"

"Whatever they calls it. You that hard up for cash, I could loan you some."

"Favor for a friend," I said, leaning over the nautical chart. "What do you know about Billy Briggs?"

"Killed a man. Whatchew lookin' for there?"

"Buried treasure, maybe," I said, laying a straightedge down on the chart and marking the spot where Harper King had staked his salvage claim. "Or maybe not. You know anything about claim-staking, Mutt. As in old offshore wrecks?"

"Some," he said, relighting a cigar that had gone out while he dozed. "Depends on if the wreck's in international waters. And with all the reefs and keys down here, that depends on where they draws the line. Gets complicated, especially if you actually bring up anything of value. Then the boys from the Bureau of Archaeological Research get all hot and bothered and they call in the lawyers, and lawyers start sharpening their pencils, and when *that* happens, bubba, you in trouble."

I left Mutt happily puffing his cigar inside a cloud of blue smoke and went to a pay phone and called Lil Cashman at home. Sammie answered. Her tone of forced gaiety convinced me she and Lil were fighting. The subject, I suspected, was m-o-n-e-y.

"Didn't we just meet," Lil said, coming on the line, "about an hour ago?"

"Sorry. A little light went on over my head, I had to call. Can you do a little research for me? Division of Archives and History."

"I'm busy. I could get someone else to do it, if it's important."

I told her it might be, and gave her the coordinates for the precise location of Harp King's wreck site.

"We're after any and all information," I said. "When the claim was filed. If it's original or a transfer from a prior claimant. You know the drill."

Lil made lawyer noises about how she would oil the gears and get the ball rolling, which presumably meant she would check out the paperwork on the claims site. Then her voice dropped into a husky register. "Stash, honey, am I pushy and domineering?"

"Absolutely," I said. "That's what I love about you."

"Sam says I'm trying to run her life. She says I'm a bully."

"Probable yes to the first," I said, trying to sound soothing. "A definite no to the second."

Lil took a deep, shuddering breath. "She says I'm worse than a man."

"No way," I said. "You don't leave the seat up."

They were expecting me back aboard *Ducat* in an hour. Time enough for a detour back to the bungalow. I fed the goldfish, watered the avocado plant, and debated whether or not to open up the war chest and smuggle a firearm back to the boat. The goldfish had nothing pertinent to say on the subject and I decided there was presently no need.

Silly me.

*   *   *

The Mallory wharf was bathed in the myriad lights emanating from *Ducat*. The old girl was decked out in all her baubles, strung from stem to stern with low-watt twinklers. She looked like a miniature aircraft carrier rigged for night landings.

"What's all the noise?" I asked Mindy.

"Some very important personage is due in from Miami," she said. "Kate is making the airport run. Harp's down in the galley. He hired a new cook."

"Billy around?"

"Search me."

"I better not," I said. "Might give me ideas."

I went below. Even with the generators running I could hear Harp King's voice booming as he chatted enthusiastically with someone in the galley.

"Murray is a veal man," he was saying. "Likes anything that's been bled white."

I had purposely left my cabin unlocked. All the better to give the impression I had nothing to hide. The drawers were built-in under the bunk, exquisite walnut cabinetry with inlaid teak details, typical of the quality finish-work throughout *Ducat*. Bronze butterfly locks kept the drawers secure when the boat was under way. I flipped them down and eased the top drawer open.

Whoever had gone through my personal belongings had been careful to keep things in order. The one mistake had been to leave a pair of socks facing the wrong way. Would Billy Briggs have been so neat? Or had it been Kate—or little Mindy, for that matter? It might, of course, have been Harp King himself, with all his talk about wanting to keep *Ducat* drug-free, but somehow I couldn't picture his wide blunt hands burrowing through my stuff. He was more the type to dump the drawer on the bunk and then stuff it all back in a jumble.

I settled myself on the bunk, hands behind my

head, and tried to puzzle it out. There was something slightly off about the whole setup, but I couldn't quite pin it down. I kept thinking about how Kate Starling looked, shivering and virtually naked, with a rare gold bracelet cupped in the palm of her hand. After a little while I started concentrating more on the naked part and less on the gold and what it meant or didn't mean. I decided it was time to pay a visit to the galley and find out who Murray the veal man was, and why he liked things that had been bled white.

"Stash, my man!"

Harp King, in white bib apron and a paper chef's hat, looked right at home in the galley. He had a meat cleaver in his right fist, a wooden hammer in his left. His gold tooth glinted as he grinned. Something Lil Cashman said made me wonder if he'd always had that tooth, or if it was part of the show, a slightly waggish come-on to the investors. When it came to attracting shareholders to such a risky venture, a romantic, piratical atmosphere was probably as important as the prospect of making big bucks. King-Ducat Salvors wasn't just an investment, it was an adventure.

He tossed me a wooden hammer. "Take a few whacks, if you don't mind," he said, indicating the raw meat on the counter. "Murray O'Shea is coming down from Miami. Old Murr's a friend of the family, so to speak, and he'll expect us to slaughter a calf in his honor."

The new cook was a boy named Paul. He was knife-blade thin with large brown eyes set wide enough apart so he had a slightly fishy look. He wore his hair in a short, swept-back cut. Modified punk, with a few of the ducktail wisps dyed orange to match the amber stone in his left earlobe. I helped him pound out a dozen veal cutlets and was not surprised to observe that the young would-be cook was intimidated to the point of stuttering by Harp, who seemed to have a professional expertise in food preparation.

"Worked my way through school doing short-order," he explained, rolling the veal in flour and spices. "After a while you get bored with flipping eggs and flapjacks. Right, Paul?"

"Y-yes, Mr. King."

"*Harp*, please. Call me mister and it makes me feel middle-aged. Come on, use your muscle, son. Pound it thin."

Paul, all wrists and elbows, flailed away with a wooden mallet. His lower lip was fat and bruised where he kept biting at it in his effort to concentrate.

I know my way around a galley but decided it was better to appear clumsy and ineffective—I didn't want to get shanghaied as a *saucier*, not when the real action was happening at seven fathoms. I finally attracted Harp's attention by dropping a piece of veal to the deck and then stumbling over it. He sighed and allowed as how I might be more useful topside.

"Paul and me got this under control, right, Paul?"

"Sure, H-h-harp."

"Maybe you can give Mindy a hand setting up the bar," he suggested, waving the cleaver cheerfully. Sweeney Todd meets Billy Budd.

Mindy was in the salon, a cozy, two-level cabin that was used for intimate entertaining. It had all the amenities, including brushed-suede upholstery, a designer-brand sound system, and original artwork in the form of stainless knickknack sculptures and flashy acrylic paintings.

Mindy had the bar stuff all squared away: bottles, mixers, glasses, ice.

"I hope they don't ask me to make the drinks," she fretted. "All I know is vodka and tonic."

I heard a car door slam and moved to the window, hoping to get a glimpse of mysterious Mr. Murray O'Shea, who expected a calf slaughtered in his honor. It was Billy Briggs climbing out of a pickup. The way he walked, springing on the balls of his feet, made me think he was high on something. When he came into the salon there was no doubt about it—his pupils remained dilated even in direct light.

"Had to go all the way to Marathon to get these mothers," he said, presenting two bottles of champagne. "Harp said Dom Perignon or nothing."

"Better ice 'em down," I told Mindy. "That stuff goes for about a buck a bubble."

Billy drifted around the cabin, rubbing a finger over his gums. "Man," he said, "you all see that purty little bracelet Kate found? Must be worth thirty, forty grand. Collectors go ape for shit like that. Next batch of investors, there's gonna be a stampede when the time comes to write out the checks."

"Like when you found the coins?" I said.

Billy concentrated on focusing his eyes. "What the hell's that s'posed to mean?"

"Nothing," I said. "Maybe I'm a little jealous. I couldn't find even a bottle cap down there."

"Bubba, you only been on the one dive, know what I'm sayin'? Ain't gonna find no motherlode the first time down."

"I guess you're right."

"You *know* I'm right," he said. Then he seemed to notice Mindy for the first time. "Ain't I right, honey? Damn if you don't look dee-licious in that slinky red dress. Good enough to eat, and that's no lie. Come on over here and give old Billy a little welcome-home kiss."

"Better not," Mindy said, keeping the bar between them. "I've got a gum infection."

I tensed, not sure how Billy would react in his present state, but he responded by having a fit of giggles. Wiping his eyes, he said, "You all hear that one, Stash? A *gum* infection? You an okay chick, Mindy. A-OK."

A horn sounded. Billy perked up. "That'll be Kate, back from the airport."

Whatever he'd been sniffing, it hadn't affected his hearing. A car door slammed. Harp's voice bellowed from the vicinity of the gangway.

"O'Shea," he roared. "You unsightly sack of sheepdip! Get your hands off my best girl and come on aboard."

I moved behind the bar and began to polish glasses. Just your average eavesdropping barkeep. The best-laid plans of an unlicensed troublemaker went astray, however, shortly after the mystery guest was escorted into the salon.

Kate Starling, leggy as always in a long silky blouse and lavender tights, had an arm around the ample waist of a balding, red-headed gentleman of about fifty. Murray O'Shea had a freckled, sunburned mug, wary, leprechaun eyes, and a bulging cowhide briefcase. He also had a definite opinion about who would tend bar.

"That's a new face," he said, squinting at me. "Harp, take care of this, please. I'm not in the mood for new faces, not after that bumpy goddamn airplane ride."

"Not to worry," Harp said. He slipped a cigar from the breast pocket of his Technicolor shirt and tossed it to me. "Right out of Fidel's humidor," he said. "Why don't you and Mindy take the night off, go out on the town or whatever? Billy can handle the bar, right, Bill?"

Billy was looking at Murray O'Shea the way a mongoose looks at a garden snake. "No problem," he said. "Can do."

Seeing as how they were giving me the bum's rush, I decided to light up the cigar and leave a little stink behind, courtesy of Señor Castro. All I got for my trouble was a faint, condescending smile from Kate Starling. Outside, in the tepid air of the open deck, I inadvertently inhaled.

Big cigar, big mistake.

Mindy pounded my back for a while. It seemed to help. When I finally stopped coughing, she said, "You look a little green around the gills, honey. You still up for a beer?"

I asked her for a rain check and coughed my way to bed.

9

AN UNNAMED low-pressure area was kicking up a fuss in the Gulf—unnamed because it hadn't yet been upgraded into a tropical storm, although you couldn't have guessed that from the size and steepness of the seas blowing offshore. Consequently Harp King, who had been closely monitoring the weather reports since dawn, decided to leave *Ducat* tethered to the wharf.

"We just have to have a little patience here, let these storms blow through," he explained after making the announcement. "No way I'm going to risk putting this vessel on the reef."

I wasn't the least disappointed. A day off suited me down to the ground. For some reason I had awoken unrefreshed, bone-weary. Maybe it was the hot wind that had piped up in the hours before dawn, and the low hum it made in the rigging. Or the uneasy sense that I was missing something fundamental about the salvage operation. Ambivalent feelings about Kate Starling didn't make sleep easy, either. Probably male ego was clouding my judgment, but I had the impression Kate was putting a lot of unnecessary effort into keeping me at arm's length—as if she felt a similar tug of attraction. Or maybe that was a head game she played with every man who crossed her path. Like Billy Briggs, for instance.

And so it went, round and round. When Harp called a lay day I tried to mask my relief. Truth was, I lacked the concentration necessary for a safe dive.

"I'm going to check my skiff," I told Mindy. "Make sure she's tied up proper."

I left her reading a paperback and wandered up Duval Street. Old Town was virtually deserted at noon. Gusts of muggy air chased last night's beer cups through the gutters. There were palm fronds down here and there, and the fickle wind was heavy with the sulfurous stink of the power plant. The bit about checking *Bushwhacked* was a fib. Instead, I cut through the side streets and fetched up on the police station.

This time the cop at the desk recognized me.

"You all the one called himself Ted Bundy."

"I suffer from a personality disorder," I said. "I'm here to see Dr. Sigmund Kerry."

The cop smirked. "Lieutenant's out to lunch."

"Better not let him hear you say that."

"Over to Pepe's," he said. "Jess don't let on I told you."

I strolled around Caroline Street and found Nelly bellied up to a café table in the little courtyard behind Pepe's. The restaurant itself was closed. There was a partially devoured take-out sandwich in a mess of waxed paper on the table, but Nelson Kerry was concentrating most of his energy on reading the sports pages of the *Miami Herald*.

"Sneaky," I said, dropping into a metal chair. "You've got the place all to yourself."

Kerry looked over the top of the paper, shaking his head. "Marino pulled a hamstring," he said. "What the hell is Shula doing, using him in exhibition?"

"Write him a letter," I suggested. "He'll appreciate your thoughts on how to coach the football team."

"Let me guess," he said. "You sought me out to tell me you were all wrong about Harp King."

"Too close to call."

Kerry folded the paper and used it to chase a cockroach from the vicinity of his sandwich. "What the hell. Doesn't a Spanish bracelet mean anything? Or did they buy it at the five-and-dime?"

"Maybe they didn't buy it at all," I said. "I'm trying to keep an open mind."

I recounted what I knew of the circumstances of the latest find.

"So you didn't actually see her find it?"

"Even if I had," I said, "it could have been planted beforehand. Very helpful for raising seed money, a find like that. Out West they used to have a technique called salting a mine. Bury some gold dust in an old shaft, bring in a potential buyer, let him make the discovery. Works like a charm."

"You're a cynic."

"Forget it, Nel. You can't hang that one on me. Taking a careful look at a quick-buck scheme doesn't make me a cynic. Cynics are people who finesse money from gullible investors. Hell," I said, "I'm the last of the romantics. I wear my heart on my sleeve."

"You haven't got any sleeves."

"Details, details. Believe it or not, I'd just as soon prove that Harper King is straight. I like the big goof. That doesn't mean we shouldn't run a background check on him."

"What do you mean 'we'?"

"You better put the cuffs on that cockroach," I said. "He's about to hijack your sandwich."

The paper came down with a bang, smearing a perfectly good headline.

"Last night we had a visitor. One Murray O'Shea, a friend of Harp's out of Miami. Five-hundred-dollar suit and a fat briefcase. If I had to guess, I'd say he's an attorney. He's got that greedy look."

"I thought one of your best friends was a lawyer."

"I'm just a bundle of contradictions, Nel. You think you could put a call into the Miami fraud squad and find out if there's any dirt on Mr. O'Shea? Five six, hundred and forty pounds, thinning red hair, fiftyish."

"Eyes?" Kerry asked, amused.

"Shifty."

"What's in it for me?"

"I'll buy you a can of Raid. You seem to be attracting a lot of wildlife."

"Son of a bitch!"

"It's the weather. Falling barometer makes 'em act crazy."

Lieutenant Kerry didn't respond. He was busy executing a complicated tap-dance on the patio tiles. I took my leaving, humming "La Curcaracha."

Back aboard *Ducat*, Mindy was catching a few rays. The new cook was nearby, peeling potatoes into a five-gallon bucket. His guilty look made me think he'd been mentally peeling the white bikini from Mindy's toffee-brown body.

"Mashed or baked," I asked.

"F-fried," he stammered.

"Mr. O'Shea like the veal cutlets?"

He nodded, dropping his eyes.

"Paul's from Minnesota," Mindy said. A visor covered most of her face. "He's only been in Key West a week and already he's got this big break. Isn't that amazing?"

I agreed. It was even more amazing that he hadn't pared off his fingertips. When I offered to help with the potatoes he relaxed and the stammer vanished. It seemed he'd hitched all the way from Minneapolis hoping to land a job in one of the better Key West restaurants, only to find it had gone out of business. He didn't bother explaining why he hadn't phoned ahead—never occurred to him, maybe. A lot of people wash up in Key West without a reasonable explanation of how they got here. Most of them drift away when the novelty wears off or the money runs out. Some, like Mutt, settle into the life.

"Harp around?" I said, feigning indifference.

"Flew up to Miami with Mr. O'Shea," Mindy said from under the visor. "Something about money."

It would be. I asked what Billy and Kate were up to.

"Taking a nap." Mindy giggled. "Separately, I assume. Billy never did get out of bed this morning. Kate went in for a siesta right after Harp left."

"That's an X-rated giggle."

"Can't help it. Not that I think old Billy Goat stands a chance. Kate's got better taste than that."

"She's also got Harp," I pointed out.

"This is true," Mindy said, sitting up. She managed to slip out of her top and turn over without revealing anything crucial. I thought I heard a fish jump, then realized it was only Paul, gulping. "Forget what I said," she said. "I was just funning."

Maybe. But I was beginning to get a sense of why *Ducat* had been rechristened *Loveboat* by the local rumor mongers. I left Mindy with her potato-peeling fan club and wandered inside. Only the gentle sigh of the air-conditioning disturbed the silence. With the cat away on business and the mice napping, it was a perfect opportunity for some shipboard snooping.

On the bridge, shielded from casual view by the smoked plexiglass windows, I changed the filter in the coffee machine and made a fresh batch. Not to drink, but as an excuse for my being there. Mindy and Paul were clearly visible on the foredeck, so I took my time and leafed through the log, looking for information on how the wreck site was first located. The handwritten entries were in felt-tip pen, a large and loopy script that seemed a reasonable reduction of the large and, to all appearances, slightly loopy captain. I smiled, noticing that he ended almost every entry with an exclamation mark.

The entry for July 14 was typical:

"Left R2 port, cleared D. Rocks. Steer 210, Vis, 8 miles!"

On that day he had taken the main shipping channel as far as the buoy marking the Eastern Dry Rocks and then steered course 210, presumably heading for the search area.

"11:45 a.m. Mag. shows poz! 1:35 p.m. Kate & B confirm ballast!"

The magnetometer, suspended by cable beneath the hull, had indicated a magnetic anomaly. The log indicated that Kate and Billy Briggs had dived to confirm the pile of ballast rocks. That was clear enough. What wasn't clear was how Harp had so accurately pinpointed his immediate search area. Backtracking from the "confirm ballast!" entry, I noted the compass headings and confirmed to my own satisfaction that Harp had been steering for a particular spot on the chart. And had found the wreck on his very first try.

The odds of doing that were as long as a moon shot. No way. The only explanation was that he had already known the exact coordinates for the wreck. Meaning someone else had to have found it first, then provided Harp with the crucial information—a fact notably absent from the video presentation. According to what he'd told the newspapers, the search for the *Rosario* wreck site had taken several weeks, focusing on a general area selected as most likely after examination of historical documents and satellite photographs.

Interesting, but not in itself evidence of fraud. Full-scale salvaging was risky, expensive work, way beyond the means of the average recreational diver. Suppose someone had spotted the pile of ballast on a weekend dive and recognized it as indication of an ancient wreck? A sport diver, aware of salvage costs, might decide to sell the information to a professional salvage outfit—maybe even keep a share of any eventual profits.

Very reasonable, really. But if that was how Harp found the site of the wreck, why didn't he just say so? Why invent the fiction of a wide-ranging search? Maybe Lily Cashman would have the answer when she reported back from the Bureau of Archaeological Research.

Down on the foredeck Paul the cook was making progress. He'd given up on peeling potatoes and was rubbing tanning lotion on Mindy's trim little back.

I returned the logbook to the slot under the helm. The vessel documentation was there, in a clear-plastic slipcase, waiting for inspection. I couldn't resist.

It showed that *Ducat* was registered to the Pulpo Development Corporation, listed at a Coral Gables address. No information as to who owned the company. I jotted down the address. Another thing for Lily Cashman to check out. If I kept it up, maybe she'd kiss off Sammie's ten grand and I could get back to the important task of breaking in my new hammock.

Down on the deck Mindy and Paul had changed places. Now she was rubbing lotion on his back. Things were looking up for the boy from Minneapolis. I emptied the cooling mug of coffee, scoured it with a dry towel, and went below, only slightly wiser.

Kate Starling was in the galley, eating raspberry sherbet out of a cardboard carton.

"Caught me in the act," she said, a smile in her cool gray eyes. "Want some?"

"Why not?"

Why not indeed? Her fluffy blonde hair had that just-showered look. The thin terry-cloth robe was loosely belted at the waist, accenting the slender line of her hips. Meanwhile the sherbet was doing nice things to her lips. The rule about not messing with another man's mate seemed silly, all of a sudden. Given half a chance, I was ready and willing to make a fool of myself.

"So you're a local," Kate said. "What do they call it, a conch?"

"That's what they call us."

We sat on opposite sides of the galley counter, knees bumping. Take it from me, there's something erotic about spooning raspberry sherbet out of the same quart, especially if your secret sharer has nothing on under her robe. Thinking about that made me warm all over. I tried to concentrate on what Kate was saying, but found myself noticing how good the raspberry lips looked, not what they were saying.

"You look like a guy who gets around," she said. "Must know all the other locals. Pardon me, conchs."

"Quite a few."

Bump-bump with the bare knees.

"Businessmen, lawyers, real-estate agents, like that?"

"Like you say, I get around."

"Mmmm," she said, lick-licking the spoon. Kate turned on the stool, bringing her thighs into contact with mine. The robe parted and I caught a glimpse of where her tan line ended. She saw me looking and smiled. My head began to feel very thick, like I was swathed in cotton.

"So," she said, placing her hands on my knees and squeezing, "when you're doing your fish-guide gig, some of your clients must be in the money, huh?"

"Sure," I said, fighting to comprehend. "Some of them. You don't have to be rich to catch a tarpon, though."

"No," she whispered, "you don't have to be rich. It'd sure be nice, though, wouldn't it?"

I agreed. I was agreeable to anything she cared to say or do. The hands on my knees slid higher as she leaned forward, bringing her lips into contact with mine. I stopped agreeing and started reacting. My eyes were closed when she suddenly backed off and said, "What I'm suggesting, Stash, is you could do yourself a favor."

"Huh?"

"Any investor you bring in, you'd get a commission."

"Yeah?"

"Yeah," she said, grinning so the pink of her tongue showed. "You can take it in shares or cash. Shares would be better, but maybe you could use a little cash, huh?"

"Let's talk about it later," I said, drawing her to me. This time her hands slipped under my shirt. The tips of her fingers stroked over my chest.

That was how Billy Briggs found us, entwined on the galley table, a few caresses shy of the ultimate act. He swore sharply, his small gray eyes instantly taking in the scene.

"Get out," he said, not looking at me. "Go on, beat it."

It all clicked into place. Billy was fresh from a shower and wearing a matching cotton bathrobe, exactly like the one Kate unhurriedly shrugged back in place, partially covering her nakedness. The look of possessive hurt he leveled at her could mean only one thing: she had come from his bed, and not long before.

Reality had a wilting effect. What was I doing even *considering* such a dumb move? I thought of myself as thoroughly adult, a grown-up in a grown-up world, but I had let the unthinking, physical part get the best of me, enough so that being compromised by Kate Starling seemed a small price to pay for a few minutes of pleasure. Cold spoons and damp knees, it all added up to a very cool play for raising more money.

Billy stepped aside and let me leave.

"We'll talk about it later," Kate called after me. "The investors, I mean. Remember, you can take the split in cash or shares."

"I'll remember," I said.

10 _____

THE NEXT day a half-ton hammerhead decided to have me for breakfast. The dive started out smooth enough. This time Harp suited up. "I'm in the mood," he said. "I feel it's my lucky day."

Mindy, who had menstrual cramps, was tending. The seas had abated somewhat, but there was still a nasty eight-foot swell that made it tricky getting into the water from the platform.

"Y'all take your time," Billy reminded us. "You want to get the rhythm. When she hits the trough between swells, keep your arms in tight and drop straight down."

After plunging in I looked up through the stream of bubbles. The bottom of *Ducat*'s hull lifted on the swell. The idea was to get well below before it came sliding down the other side. My ears started popping. I swallowed rapidly, equalizing the pressure. The air was clean and sweet, delivered by the reassuring *clunk* of the regulator.

I touch bottom first. Billy and Harp came down together, buddied up for the first part of the dive. In his black wet suit Harp looked like a walrus that had sprouted legs. Then another, slimmer figure pierced the rippled mirror at the top of the world. The golden girl herself, Kate Starling. This time I vowed to be watching if and when she uncovered another chunk of precious metal.

Kate was carrying a camera, the better to record the undersea exploits of King-Ducat Salvors. Two strobes emerged from the clear-plastic housing. She popped the flash, testing, and for a moment the bottom was pink, the schooling yellowtails bright yellow. Harp's mask was blood-red and the whites of his eyes glowed like headlamps. Then the strobe faded and the undersea world returned to shades of green and gray.

I noticed Harp's movements were slow and assured. No sign of panic. A single-shot bang stick dangled from his wrist. A confidence builder, I thought, no harm in that.

Little did I know.

We followed Billy and his directional locator to the wreck site. The approach was from a different angle. The ballast stones loomed suddenly, higher than I remembered, as if the bottom current had cleared away some of the sand. For the first time I was able to discern the remains of ship timbers crushed under the stones. Only fibrous strands remained, morsels the teredo worms had found inedible. Maybe the timbers belonged to the *Rosario* or the *San Mateo,* and maybe not. It would take more than a few coins and a single bracelet to convince me.

"We got her cornered," Harp had announced the night before, returning from Miami with an appraisal of the bracelet. "It's the *Rosario,* all right, I can feel it in my bones. All we gotta do, we gotta find those bronze cannon and the gold bars will be right alongside, probably stacked just like it was in the hold. Five hundred bars, twenty pounds per. *You* figure it out!"

Ten thousand pounds of gold would net roughly fifty million dollars at current prices. Maybe a lot more if the bars were brought up by collectors who coveted the Spanish foundry marks. It was a nice

round figure, fifty million. It concentrated the mind
wonderfully. Even wealthy Palm Beach investors
tended to smile, hearing it.

Billy assigned me a new set of quadrants to the
east of the ballast pile. Right away it was different.
The needle on the detector gauge jumped as soon as
I put it near the bottom. Too easy, I thought, must
be a malfunction. I lifted the plate away from the
bottom. The needle declined, then jumped again
when I brought it down.

When that happens, you start to argue with yourself. Can't be anything, you say, equipment must be
screwedup. Your heart is thumping away and in
the back of your mind is this faint golden glow,
coloring the way you think.

The detector was equipped with a small blower
about the size and power of a hair dryer, only designed to move water. It had a slight kick. I dug my
fins into the bottom, holding in place. The sand
lifted away, leaving the heavier pebbles. I swept the
blower over a tight area, creating a shallow depres-
sion. All at once the round shapes started popping
up through the bottom, like the blackened tops of
buried eggs. I switched off the blower and pried one
of the "eggs" out of the sand. Round and heavy,
part of it crumbled in my hand. Not gold or bronze,
certainly. Iron, maybe. Musket balls or grapeshot for
the cannons. I turned the blower back on, playing it
over a wider area. The eggs were everywhere, just
beneath the surface.

I thought, Where there's cannon balls there must
be . . . And then it smashed into me from behind. A
force like a giant hand flinging me forward. Something large and powerful tried to tear the scuba
tanks from my back. My regulator popped out of my
mouth, and with it my air.

My precious air.

The emergency regulator was right there on my vest, clipped to the BC valve. Never thought of it. Wanted the regulator that had been torn away. Reached behind my head, searching. Hand hit something big and solid and sharp. Jerked my hand away, saw green stuff pouring from my fingers. Green stuff? Red looks green at forty feet. Blood.

Blood? Blood! Mine!

I was jerked sideways, violently. There was a god-awful crunching noise, a ferocious scratching. Like fingernails on slate. Teeth on aluminum. The straps tore away and the tank rack came partway off my back. I craned my head, aware that my mask was starting to flood. A few inches away a gray, bony thing was looking at me with an unblinking eye.

My brain supplied the unwanted information: shark. Hammerhead shark. Then it was gliding over my shoulder, an immense, endless bulk. A zigzagging express train, airbrushed gray. It had mechanical, herky-jerky movements.

Thrashing. Which meant it was attacking, intending to feed.

My hand closed on the regulator. I must have put it into my mouth because air jetted into my burning lungs. The big tail fin smacked the side of my head.

The hammer was turning, coming back.

The tanks came loose. I grabbed the rack, holding the scuba tanks out in front of me. Hiding.

It was coming back.

I discovered you can scream into a regulator and gulp air at the same time. The shark came straight at me, all teeth and fins and elongated eye bones. The open jaws locked on the tanks, driving me backward. My mask came off. My eyes burned with the salt. I was naked, defenseless. I tried to shrink. More than anything I wanted to be smaller than the tanks. Then the jaws opened and the hammer thrashed on by. I sank to the bottom and tried to burrow under the tanks. I knew it was turning, coming back.

Only it didn't. What grabbed me was a pair of human hands. I grabbed back. Someone pushed a flooded mask over my eyes. A regulator purged the water and the mask was roughly shoved back in place. A faceplate pressed against my mask. I could see eyes.

It was Harper King, holding my shoulders with his big, strong hands. I didn't get it. What was he doing near me? Did he want to be shark food, too? Didn't he know the hammerhead was coming back?

Harp made a sign, urging me to watch the way his hand moved. Okay—that was the sign. *Okay.*

The hell it was.

He nodded, showing me the bang stick. Waving it like a magic wand. As indeed it had been. Then another pair of hands took hold of me. Smaller hands. Kate. Then the two of them were conspiring, urging me to do something.

Go up. That was the sign. Eventually I understood. I remember thinking, as they guided me up, ascending slowly and deliberately toward the surface, that it was nice having two humans next to me. Maybe the shark would eat one of them instead.

Mindy brought me a mug of something hot. It was eighty-five degrees on deck and I was shivering. It was hard to hold the mug because my right hand was wrapped in a bulky red bandage.

"How many'd he get?"

"Go on, drink it," Mindy said.

Ducat was under way, cutting an angle through the swells.

"How many?" I said. "Tell me, please."

"He's worried about his hand."

That was Harp's voice. Then he was crouching beside me, saying. "You got a mean slice, right to the bone. But I counted five fingers. All you need is a few stitches, be as good as new."

I nodded. I didn't believe him, exactly, but I wasn't ready to open the bandage and find out. "Who's driving the boat?"

"Billy," he said. "I'm playing doctor. That compress hurt?"

I hadn't noticed the compress tied around my upper arm. Cutting off the blood to my hand. Just like in the first-aid manual.

"That was one big son of a bitch," he said. "Must have a taste for scuba tanks, huh?"

"What?" I was more interested in the way Harp's gold tooth caught the light than in what he had to say.

"I think he's in shock," Mindy said.

"Am not."

"Put this blanket around him."

"Must have been the same shark," Harp said. "Went for your tanks, just like it went for mine."

"You killed it."

"Them bang sticks come in handy," he said. "Old Mr. Shark never knew what hit him."

Harp, working a quadrant nearby, had seen the hammer coming directly at me from behind. No circling, he said, but a charge straight at the tanks. The blower had been raising a cloud of sand, which made it difficult to see clearly. Harp swam up over me, and when the shark let go of the tanks for the second time, he got close enough to jam the bang stick down on its head.

"It was the damnedest thing." he said. "Shark tilts a little, like a truck with two flat tires. Then it kind of swims sideways, thrashing around, and attempts to bury its head in the sand. Then it stops moving, like a switch clicked off inside. Billy says other sharks probably et it up by now."

My heart was beginning to thud a little less violently. I could feel where my hand was cut, and that was good; not feeling had been frightening.

"Grapeshot," I said. "Or musket ball."

Harp laughed. "You're talking crazy, Stash. It was a bang stick got him. Twelve-gauge shotgun slug."

"No," I said. "On the bottom. Hundreds of them. About the size of an egg."

It didn't take long for Harper King to appreciate the significance. His way of demonstrating enthusiasm was to make deep whooping noises while executing a shuffling, sideways step. Dance of the golden bear.

"Sum bitch!" he roared. "We found the cannon!"

After giving me a hug that nearly crushed the air from my chest he bounded up the ladder to the bridge, proclaiming gold in them thar hills, or something to that effect.

"You look a little pale," Mindy said. She got on her knees behind me and used her warm hands to massage my neck muscles. "You're all tensed up."

"Being an appetizer does that to me."

After a while the cords in my neck began to relax.

"Kate took pictures," Mindy said. "Can you believe that?"

"Explain."

"When you got attacked. She had the camera and she took pictures. A whole roll on motor-drive, she said."

Somehow it didn't surprise me. The lady had the nerves of a combat photographer. "This is Kate Starling, live from Beirut." Mindy thought she should have dropped the camera and come to my rescue. I didn't agree.

"Harp had the weapon," I said. "It was his move.

If Kate tried anything, she might be missing a limb or two."

"I suppose so."

Ducat was clearing Whitehead Spit. There were a few diehard sunbathers on the shore by the fort, risking melanoma on an August afternoon. Flesh baked, as dry and brown as Gucci leather. I was definitely feeling better. High, almost. Being alive was a drug in itself. I wiggled my fingers inside the bandage and counted five.

"Your tanks are goners," Mindy said.

I looked at the wreck of chewed aluminum. Might be able to salvage the regulator, have it rebuilt. I found a triangle of thin white bone embedded in the harness rack. A shark tooth. I pried it loose. Souvenir of a jitterbug with death. A good-luck piece. Looking for another tooth, I noticed something that spoiled my mood. Something that explained why the hammerhead had been so interested in eating my tanks and me, since I happened to have them strapped to my back.

It was a fish, a red snapper to be exact. Cut open and wedged into the narrow gap between the two tanks. There's nothing that stimulates a shark's appetite like the scent of a disemboweled fish. And as far as the hammerhead had been able to discern, the delicious smell had been coming from me.

I didn't like it. I never like it when someone tries to murder me.

11 _____

LIEUTENANT NELSON Kerry was blowing smoke. He paused to glance at the clean gauze covering the stitches on my right hand and said, "Only a damn fool sticks his fingers into a shark's mouth."

I sighed. Nelly always get obstreperous when he's given up on quitting cigarettes. Makes him mean and mouthy. "You're avoiding the question," I said.

"It hurt much?"

"Itches like crazy. What hurts is my boyhood chum has certain information he doesn't want to share."

The smoke rings resumed. Translucent blue doughnuts of smoke punctuated the slant of morning light that filled Kerry's office.

"I have access to certain information," he said, "because I am a duly appointed public servant. You, on the other hand, are a civilian. In addition to being a damn fool."

"Thanks for clearing that up, Nel," I said. "What I'd like to know, are you interested in the fact somebody tried to kill me?"

Kerry smiled. It was not a happy smile. It was a I-hate-myself-because-I-can't-kick-the-butts smile. "What do you want?" he said. "You want me to arrest the shark? Oh, I forgot, the shark is dead. Too bad, it might have made a good witness."

I decided to wait him out. Nelson Kerry is basically a hell of a good guy and I knew he'd do the right thing. Part of the problem was the month's salary he'd invested in King-Ducat Salvors. He didn't want to kiss it good-bye or admit he'd been taken in by a professional grifter. No one does, especially not a duly appointed public servant who is in a position to know better.

"Maybe you should get a hook," he said, indicating the bandage. "How about a matching eye patch? Think what a hit you'd be at the Green Parrot. The girls would love it."

I closed my eyes and pretended to snore.

"Okay," Kerry said. "I give up. Harper King did time. Got mixed up in a stock-option scheme. The usual boiler-room operation. Small office, bank of phones, several bank accounts. His specialty was dentists. What Harp did was phone dentists in the Lauderdale area and tell each and every one this exciting inside information about a stock that was hot hot hot."

"Let me guess," I said. "The stock didn't actually exist."

That made Nelson Kerry happy. "Wrong," he said. "It existed and it was in fact hot. Only old Harp didn't know it. See, he was taking money from the tooth fairies and their various spouses and girlfriends. Only he never got around to buying the options because he figured the stock was a dog, they'd all have lost money on paper when the option came due."

"Ouch."

"Exactly. For a three-month period the dough for just about every root-canal job in Broward County went into Harper King's pocket. Then one of the dentists finally stopped sniffing nitrous oxide long enough to figure out he didn't actually have any options, only these little blue receipts that were worth maybe eight cents. He goes to the SEC and the SEC turns him over the the FBI and the FBI puts a wire on him, this pissed-off dentist, and he goes to see Harper King in person, to inquire as to why he can't seem to cash in his options for all the money he supposedly has coming. And Harp, who apparently loves the sound of his own voice, he says enough stuff so his private parts are firmly thumbtacked to the cork board, if you know what I mean."

"I get the idea."

"Wait," he said. "It gets better. Guess who sold almost as many phony options as Mr. Big Mouth?"

"Murray O'Shea."

"Wrong again," he said. "But close. Lady name of Katherine Starling."

I had that old sinking feeling, like when the elevator comes to a stop and your stomach keeps on going down, way past Ladies' Lingerie, all the way to the basement, down, down.

"O'Shea was King's defense attorney," Kerry said. "Pleaded him to a deal before it came to trial. Part of the deal, the reason King had to do time, he took it on the chin. Said it was all his idea, he was the only one knew the options hadn't actually been purchased. So all that happened to Ms. Starling, the SEC suspended her securities license for a year. No one seemed overly concerned she was sharing Harp's place of domicile, might have been in a position to know he was gassing the tooth fairies."

"He's a stand-up guy," I said.

"As con men go, yeah, I guess you could say that. Also he's a super salesman, the kind of mouth can convince an Eskimo what he really needs, to make the igloo comfy, is central air-conditioning. Which makes me just another Key West Eskimo, huh?"

"I wouldn't say that, Nel," I said. "Maybe there really is treasure down there. Maybe Harp wants to strike it rich so he can pay back all the people he defrauded."

"Did I say he defrauded people?" Kerry snorted. "I said 'dentists.' This is a separate and distinct species. Which you will understand, you ever call one on a weekend, you happen to be in great pain."

It didn't seem prudent to mention that there were those who considered cops a separate species, similarly indifferent to pain and suffering.

"Anyhow," Kerry said. "You're only sticking up for Harp because you think he saved your life."

"I was dead meat, Nel. Shark bait."

"And you think it was Billy Briggs set you up. Pissed off because you put a move on Kate Starling, who is supposed to be the love of Harp King's life. I mean, is it any wonder I'm having trouble following this alleged attempt on your life? You don't have any evidence, you just have this gut feeling."

"It's a theory."

"You know what they called Briggs up in the Raiford Correctional Facility? Called him 'Mugsy,' on account of the weapon he used to kill his buddy who had the misfortune to be married to the woman Briggs was boffing. Cute, huh?"

"That where Harp and Billy got acquainted? Raiford?"

Kerry shook his head. "Nah, King did his stretch in the federal lockup. The connection is, he and Billy happen to have the same attorney. The one you said like to eat baby cows—Murray O'Shea—whose clientele is made up exclusively of clients who have committed crimes for which they would rather not be convicted. This is an attorney likes to avoid having to discuss things with a jury if at all possible. Waste of his valuable time. Like he pleaded Briggs down from second to third degree. And the deal he worked for King, making sure the love of his life was free to visit him and bring him clean socks and stuff. Or the deal he worked for Freddie Del Ray, so he could skip out on the two-million bail he posted."

"Whoa, Nellie," I said. "Back it up. Freddie who?'

"Del Ray. First name Fernando, except up in the Boca Raton Country Club they preferred Freddie because it didn't sound so, you know, *foreign*. Del Ray owned a couple of banks. Not the kind you stand in line to deposit your paycheck and get a free toaster. Investment banks. Very hot these days, investment banks. Also he owned his own offshore mutual fund, which as near as the FBI could determine was actually not a mutual fund but merely a post-office box in the Cayman Islands. That's how come Freddie had to put up two-million bail so he could take an extended vacation on the Caribbean island he happens to own down there, which he bought with the proceeds of the mutual fund that was really a P.O. box. Are you following this?"

"I'm dazzled."

"Yeah, well, Freddie dazzled a lot of people up at the country club. Very social. Charities, Republican fund-raisers. He played, you know, polo and stuff. That's where you ride around on a pony and hit this little white ball?"

"I'm confused," I said. "We were talking about Murray O'Shea and now we're playing polo. What's the connection?"

Kerry ground the cigarette butt in a glass ashtray. The squeaking noise made my teeth hurt. "The connection is that one of the Del Ray's investment banks owned Harper King, or to exact they owned the securities license Harp was using when he told fibs to all those dentists."

"Boy oh boy," I said. "It sure is a small world, ain't it?"

*   *   *

They were winching some new equipment aboard *Ducat*. Billy Briggs stood on deck, directing the crane. Seeing me, he grinned and made a thumbs-up. What a pal. I decided to play it cool, as if I'd never found the bait jammed in my scuba tanks.

"Can you still dive?" he wanted to know.

"Soon as the stitches come out. What's this?" I asked, looking at the coils of black hose.

"Airlift. You found those cannonball, Harp got a hard-on for an airlift, leased this sucker out of Marathon. Them little blowers won't cut it, not if something's buried deep."

Mindy and Kate Starling were in the salon, setting up for another investment presentation. It was on the tip of my tongue to ask Kate how she had felt about delivering clean underwear to her boyfriend when he was on his enforced vacation. Did they hold hands through the wire mesh in the visitor's room, or what? Instead, I let Mindy fuss over my hand.

"Mean old beast."

"Oh, I'm not that old," I said. "Or that mean."

"I meant the shark, silly. Don't you take *anything* serious?"

Kate smiled indulgently, implying Mindy was a mere flirting girl. "I'm sure he has his secrets," she said. "Right, Stash?"

"Sure," I said. "By day I dive for Spanish gold. By night I stalk the mean streets, biting victims on the neck."

"How exciting for you," Kate said, deadpan.

Mindy asked if I'd seen the new airlift.

"Looks expensive," I said.

"Harp says it's worth every penny. He says now they'll know we're serious."

Kate gave her a killing look. I didn't know what part she didn't like, the airlift being expensive or the "they" who might doubt the seriousness of the venture. Maybe both. She changed the subject by mentioning the "presentation" scheduled for that evening.

"We want you there, Stash," she said. "We have a major investor who is thinking of doubling up, now that we have tangible evidence. You can tell her about finding the layer of grapeshot. And of course the encounter with the hammerhead. A whiff of danger makes us that much more attractive, don't you agree?"

"Oh, absolutely," I said. "And you got it all on film, right?"

"I got a few shots, yes," she said, caught off guard.

"I can't wait. Right now, if it's okay, I've got a few personal errands?"

She waved bye-bye, batting eyes that were impassive and cool. Very cool indeed.

12 _____

I CLEARED the fallen palm fronds off the coupe and backed it into the street, where I eased the top down. The upholstery was patched with duct tape, covering the machete cuts made by a certain unpleasant individual, since deceased. Other than the slashes in the leather and the rust-blistered trunk lid and the usual dings and scratches, the old Coupe de Ville was in prime shape. She had thirty-gallon fuel tank, a big V-8, stereo speakers with a fat sound, whitewall sneakers, cruise control, and a remarkable pair of tail fins. The muffler had a bad cough, but there was hope for recovery.

There was always hope. Hope that Mr. Benjamin T. Jones would be at his domicile on Sugarloaf Key. Hope that Lily Cashman's information about Mr. Jones being the previous owner of the *Rosario* claim site was accurate. Hope that no officer of the law would notice that my plates had expired.

I put a tape in the deck, cranked the volume up until Annie Lennox sounded like she was singing from the back seat, and steered with my left hand. No problem. It was a straight run to Sugarloaf, mostly.

The Florida Keys, for those who haven't had the pleasure, are a string of low mangrove islands extending like a scorpion tail southwest from the mainland, the barb end being Key West. Before Flagler built his crazy railroad the only method of transportation from one key to the next was by steamer or sail. Flagler fixed that. Then, after his railroad got blown out in '37, they built the Overseas Highway, a two-lane strip of bridges that runs just above sea level, a hundred and thirty miles out into the Gulf.

In season, when the snowbirds come in their campers and rented cars, the traffic is bumper-to-bumper. On a muggy afternoon in the hurricane month of August, I had the road pretty much to myself. Gray clouds boiled along the horizon, a reminder of the dirty weather offshore, but overhead the sky was deep and blue. The sea was milky green, the color of tarnished brass, darker where the turtle grass grew on the shallow bottom.

I found the Paradise Mobile Park on the Atlantic side of the key. The name Ben Jones was scrawled on a mailbox, one of twenty or so staked at the entrance. A ragged-looking canal had been chopped through the park. Rows of unkempt coconut palms delineated the trailer sites. According to the number on the mailbox, Jones lived on the other end of the canal. I parked the coupe in the shade and walked.

A pit bull shot out from under one the trailers and stopped short at the end of a tether, teeth bared. The tether was strong length of galvanized chain; just as well, since climbing palm trees is pretty tough one-handed.

"I'm go shoot that dawg, someday."

The drawling voice came from a screened porch. Up closer I could just make out an old man in a rocker. "Ben Jones?" I asked.

"Who wants him? You come here peddlin' assurance, I don't want none."

"I'm looking for gold," I said. "Treasure from the *Rosario*. You got any?"

The old man laughed. I couldn't see him very well in the shadow of the screen, but the laugh helped. It said he would have a rascal face.

"Shee-it," he said. "Y'all come on in heah and sit by me."

I went up the rickety steps. Jones looked to be in his late seventies. It was hard to be sure, with what whiskey and weather had done to him. I was right about the rascal face, although mostly it was in the eyes now, a dare-me squint that had surely been there when he was a boy.

"Gonna blow out there," he said. "I been watchin' the way the sky moves. Bad stuff comin'."

I agreed that the weather was iffy. I had the feeling he knew exactly what I was after, that there was no point trying to hustle or hurry him. The old man kept a picnic cooler of beer close to his chair. A sinewy arm dipped into the cooler and drew out two cans of a discount brand.

"This here's breakfus', lunch, an' supper," he said, popping the tab. "Never liked grits no how. An' my teef, dey *long* gone." He laughed at himself, then looked me over, head to toe. He noticed the bandage but didn't comment. "You a waterman, son?"

I admitted to fish-guiding when I couldn't get honest work.

"I can always tell a waterman. Walk on the ball of the feets, up on the toes, finding that water balance." He sipped leisurely at the beer, like an ancient grouper nuzzling a feed hole in the reef. "I hate to disappoint you, son, but I already done sold the *Rosario* claim."

We talked, trading bits of information. Getting Ben Jones to come to the bait was like laying down a chum line a few morsels at a time. He was willing to take the hook, but at his own speed, in his own way.

"Great big fella," he said, referring to Harper King. "Friendly as all get-out. Like to blow the walls down, with that big voice he got. And talk? It was beautiful, hearing him go on so. I could tell he didn't know boats, nor the local waters. Flat-footed, like a honey bear. I took his money, though— yes'em, I did do that. The way I figure, five thousand dollah buy ten thousand can a beer, give or take. Enough to keep me wet for six, seven years. By which time I won't *need* no more beer."

"Five grand?" I said. "That's all?"

The old turtle eyes hardened. "Son, you come in the springtime, I'd a traded that claim for a bottle of five-dollar rum. Which is five dollars more'n she's worth. Ain't no Spanish gold down there. Never was."

"Does Harper King know that?"

Ben Jones rocked in the chair, cradling the beer can in his crab-claw hands. "I tol' him, but I cain't swear he listen. That big fella, he a man who only hear what he want. An' what he want was title to a wrecked galleon. *Any* wrecked galleon. I tol' him, I say, 'What you want, the famous plate ship *Rosario* hit the reef of Matecumbe. The *Rosario* sunk off Key West, that another ship entire.' "

"Plate ship?"

He nodded. "Gold plate, tons of it. Had ten thousands pounds of indigo dye on board, with the gold hidden in the dye. Hoping to fool the Dutch pirates, maybe. Never mind. She done hit the reef and went down in six fathoms. Real slow like, so they was able to mark the spot. The indigo helped, the way it kept bleeding out. Spanish salvors came back the next year and got most of the gold plate back up to the surface. What they did, they used slave divers. Load them slaves down with a big rock, throw 'em over the side, they had best come up with something shiny. Mighty primitive salvage technique. Went through a lot of slaves." He grinned, liking the idea, and slurped at his beer. "But what happened, they recovered the best part of the plate. Not all of it, though, and none of the gold coin. A hundred thousand doubloon, that's still down there, somewhere off the Matecumbe reef. Buster Sawyer, up Islamorada way, he been working that claim site for years. Never got him more than a dozen coins, but he still a believer. Oh yes."

I asked what he meant about another ship named *Rosario*. He laughed, shaking his wobbly head. "Oh, Lord, that was a good joke on Buster, and on me, too, a course. Two ships called the same, only they sunk more'n fifty years apart. One rich as Croesus, the other full of nothin' but ballast rock and stone cannonball. You gotta understand, son, what the prospect of findin' gold does to a man's brain. Don't matter how reasonable he be, once the idea of treasure takes hold, he no better than yer average looney. All he think about is the gold, how he gonna find it. It ain't the making him rich he crave, it the sight of that gold, lyin' there at the bottom of the sea."

In the sunlit park the pit bull was frothing at the end of the chain, eyes as cold as beads of glass.

"Buster'd read about the *Rosario* and the idea hooked him. Searched the Matecumbe reef for three, four years, never found more'n a few coins. Then he hears about this Key West shrimper, hooked his nets on a bronze cannon. Now the plate ship had bronze cannon. Lots of galleons did, but Buster gets it in his head to check out this cannon the shrimpers got hold of, and lo and behold, he finds the numbers inscribed on the cannon match those of a ship called *Rosario*. He knew from the Archive manifest it couldn't be the same ship, but he just plain wouldn't believe it. Date was wrong, place was wrong, cargo was wrong. Had to be the wrong wreck. Didn't matter to Buster. Spent two years blasting holes in the sand all around that wreck site, never found nothing but a few bronze cannon and a useless bunch of stone cannonball. Which only made sense, since the *Rosario* that sunk off Key West was *loaded* with cannonball, 'cording to what was writ in the Archive of the Indies. That was her *cargo*. She weren't no treasure ship. Buster knew that. I knew that. But we had the gold fever, son. We just plain wanted to believe.''

I knew the feeling. Not in the gold fever, but in wanting to believe in Harper King.

''I'm even dumber than Buster Sawyer,'' the old man said with a sense of profound satisfaction. ''Watched him work that pile of ballast for two years. When he give it up, I was there on his doorstep, just itching to buy that claim site. A thousand dollars, that's what I give 'im. An' that was only the beginning. Had me some acreage in Homestead, an' I sold that and hired me a boat and scuba divers and we managed to dribble another fifty thousand into that useless pile of rocks. Oh, it was a lovely time. Every day, that was going to be the day we uncovered them chests of gold coin. Son, it was better'n bein' in love. It was romance.''

I nodded. I knew about romance, too. ''What do you suppose Harper King wants with that wreck?'' I asked.

Ben Jones thought about it a while. ''Could be,'' he said finally, ''he found him a new way to get money off'n the ocean floor.'' He smiled, showing bare gums. It was a notion he approved of, making money out of nothing but blue sky and green water. ''But don't pay no attention to no old fool like me. I ain't no smarter'n that dawg out there, all the time fightin' hisself on the chain.''

I kept my distance going back. I was fed up with critters that wanted to bite me. Soon enough it would be time to bare my own teeth, such as they were.

*   *   *

The Germans were laying seige to Mutt Durgin's bait shack. Two large yellow-headed boys who looked to be brothers. Their English was precise and earnest.

"Vee would haff tarpon. You find us tarpon, yes, please?"

Mutt was hiding under his palm-frond sombrero. When he saw me, his teeth showed white.

"Stash, come here and talk to these hombres. They won't take no for an answer."

"Stash?" Recognizing the name posted on the shack, one of the brothers pointed to where *Bushwhacked* was warped to the pilings. "You are skiff guide, you make us catch tarpon, yes?"

I held up my damaged hand. "Sorry, fellas. War wound. You go on over to Garrison Bight, find the *Chaser*. Ask for Mike Wilbur. If there are tarpon on the flats, he'll find 'em for you."

The Germans retreated politely. Mutt sighed. "Heck of a thing, when a man has to refuse money on account his only client is too busy playing with sharks to earn an honest living."

I told Mutt about the planted baitfish that had drawn the hammerhead to me. His eyes narrowed.

"These boys playing hardball, T.D. Maybe what I should do, sign on that *Loveboat* and keep an eye on you."

"I'll be fine. Things are coming together."

"Yeah, I can see that," Mutt said. "You got 'em stitched together, all bandaged up."

"It's a con, all right," I said, ignoring him. "I just need to find an angle, a way to get Sammie's money out from under before the pyramid collapses."

Mutt muttered about dangling angles and damn fools as I followed him into the bait shack. "Here," he said. "Lily come by this morning, left this for you."

I opened the envelope.

Checked out Pulpo Development, Coral Gables. One of many fronts controlled by Fernando Del Ray. Urgent that you call me.

L.

I liked it. It had balance. It had symmetry. The *Ducat* was owned by Freddie Del Ray, an embezzler represented by criminal attorney Murray O'Shea. The *Ducat* was now leased to Harper King, a con artist represented by criminal attorney Murray O'Shea. Divemaster on the *Ducat* was Billy Briggs, a killer represented by criminal attorney Murray O'Shea.

Old Murray got around. He was under a lot of different rocks. "Criminal attorney" was starting to sound like an apt description. And I was willing to bet the stitches on my right hand that Freddie Del Ray wasn't loaning Harper King the *Ducat* out of the goodness of his heart.

"I'm serious," Mutt said. "You go back on that boat, you better watch your ass."

"No need," I said. "I got several people watching it for me."

13

THE SLIDE show was a big hit. Mrs. Bertram was so impressed they ran through the sequence a second time. She had been in the group of investors down from Palm Beach the first night I was aboard. Now she was back alone, drawn by the discovery of the bracelet. She had a thing for jewelry. I recognized her by the multitude of pearls and the large diamond brooch pinned to her bosom. She recognized me by the bandage.

"Look at the *size* of him," she said. "Marvelous."

It was the shark who had the marvelous size, not me. Kate had kept the motor-drive camera smoking for the duration of the attack. The first few shots were of Harp, mugging for the camera. Holding his metal detector and pointing to the sandy bottom. Then there was a shot of him swimming out of the frame, kicking up a swirl of dust with his power fins.

From then on the hammerhead and I shared the feature roles. The camera had clicked off a frame every second or so. The sequence of slides had the effect of a stop-action film. I was on the bottom, pushed forward, and the shark was gnawing at my tanks. Yum yum. You could see the awkward tilt of the open jaws, the rows of teeth grinding into the aluminum, the weird, winglike head bone of the shark. You could see its expressionless eyes. You could see, in quite a few of the shots, my very expressive eyes, bugging out behind my mask.

My hand, trailing blood.

Red blood, the color rendered accurate by Kate's strobe flash. In one slide I was being upended by the flick of the tail. I don't remember that happening, but there it was on screen, almost as big as life. There was also a really evocative shot of me curled up in a fetal position, trying to bury myself in the sand.

"How terrifying!" Mrs. Bertram exclaimed. She sounded delighted. "Can you back up, I want to see that one again."

"You don't mind, do you, Stash?" Harp said. It wasn't really a question. Mrs. Bertram was thinking seriously about picking up a significant investment in the salvage company. Big bucks. Harper King gave the impression he would quite willing get down on all fours and play Rover if that's what tickled Mrs. Bertram's fancy.

So we watched me get mauled, and then we watched it again. In forward, reverse, in luminous Ektachrome. After a while my hand started to itch. Then the back of my neck. I remembered—how had I forgotten?—what the force of displaced water felt like as the great body rushed at me. The sensation of helpless panic in my hummingbird heart.

"No, I don't mind," I said. "I'll just help myself to a little drink."

All the while—for the whole of the evening, for that matter—I could feel Kate Starling's eyes appraising me. Probably wondering how much I knew. And I, in turn, wondered if she had been in on the fish-baiting incident. The vicarious thrill of the shark encounter was selling Mrs. Bertram, that much was obvious. Could I have been set up merely to add a little spice to the sales pitch?

That would mean Harp was in on the trick, had come equipped with the bang stick prepared to effect a last-second rescue.

I poured myself a healthy dose of Kentucky bourbon and watched the big guy making his pitch to the lady with the diamond brooch. I decided the best candidate was still Billy Briggs, out of jealousy or maybe even sheer perversity. Hating me because he remembered enough of his humiliation at the Pirates Den to seek revenge. Wanting to scare me away from Kate, and from *Ducat*.

Yes, it had to be Billy. That made a lot more sense than the notion of Harp King risking his life for a slide show. It would have been interesting to observe Billy's reaction to the pretty pictures on the screen, but old fishbait Bill had taken a powder. Jumped ship for the evening. Out on the prowl, according to what he'd told Mindy.

"Said he was going to get candy," Mindy had said, mystified.

I knew what that meant. Candy was Cindy Ann, the kootch dancer. My first reaction was to figure she and Briggs deserved each other. And then I thought, No one deserves Billy Briggs, least of all a harmless little stripper whose only sin was providing dry thrills for wet-behind-the-ears Coast Guard recruits. If sin it was. I'd been living in a glass house long enough so I was reluctant to rear back and throw, rockwise.

The lights came on. Mrs. Bertram applauded.

Harp said, "Stash, get yer butt on over here."

I got on over, holding the glass in my left hand. Mrs. Bertram was beaming at Harp and he was beaming at me. There was a lot of good feeling going on. An essential ingredient when one is promoting large sums of cash money.

"What we're not forgetting," Harp said, "is it was

Stash found the layer of grapeshot. Them bronze cannon are bound to be in close proximity. Now, I'm here to tell you I *know* what it feels like to be breakfast in the eyes of one of them powerful varmints, and I got just the cure for it, too. Kate, honey?"

Kate honey handed him a long skinny box, done up in paper and ribbons.

"This here is the magic wand," he said, handing the box to me. "All you got to do is wave it and *poof!* the sharks disappear."

I unwrapped the box.

"That there is the very best repellent money can buy. All he's gotta do, Mrs. Bertram, is poke that bang stick at the head and good-bye, Mr. Hammerhead. Or Mr. Tiger Shark, or whoever."

I hefted the weapon, made sure the breech was empty, and tested the spring action. It felt good in my hands. No doubt it was the power of suggestion that made my stitches stop itching. I thanked Harp and meant it.

"Will you dive again?" Mrs. Bertram wanted to know. She seemed faintly amused at the idea.

"Soon as my fingers heal."

"He's dying to get back down there," Harp said, oblivious to the irony. "Right, Stash?"

"Right," I said. "Me and my new magic wand."

Later, when I had time to reflect on it, I decided they had been saving Murray O'Shea for the closing. He didn't make his appearance until after the last of the crab claws had been cracked and the coffee served. Paul, the new cook, had done himself proud. He wore a white chef's hat while serving. If Mrs. Bertram noticed the purple tufts of his punk hairdo, she didn't comment. With Harp keeping up a steady barrage of treasure-hunting anecdotes, distraction from the main event was unlikely.

O'Shea made his entrance as Harp was telling a

very large fib about how he and Kate had narrowed down the galleon search area after painstaking research in the Archive of the Indies. He didn't explain how he'd acquired an expertise in deciphering seventeenth-century Spanish. Mrs. Bertram either didn't pick up on the discrepancy or didn't care.

"There it was, wrapped in that old moldy bundle, the manifest of the *Rosario*. I was stunned, absolutely stunned. Eight *months* of searching through jumbled manuscripts!" he exulted. "Eight months of doubt and frustration. And we'd *found* it, proof positive that the ship existed. Tears of joy came to my eyes, isn't that right, Kate?"

But Kate was already on her feet, greeting O'Shea as he bustled into the salon and plunked his briefcase unceremoniously on the dinner table.

"I swear to you," he announced. "I am never again boarding a small aircraft."

"Murray gets airsick," Harp confided to Mrs. Bertram. "Seasick, too. I just been telling Mrs. Bertram all about our trials and tribulations at the Archive. 'Course, being a tax lawyer you know all about the paper chase, don't you, Murray?"

O'Shea agreed that he did indeed. He slumped into a chair and accepted a double vodka.

"Airplanes," he sighed. "You better find this gold quick, Harp. These sudden commutes from Miami are killing me. I left my stomach somewhere over Key Largo."

"Try some bitters and soda," Mrs. Bertram advised. "Settles the gut. My Henry had tummy troubles and he swore by Angostura bitters."

O'Shea made a face, but he downed the pink concoction, which I prepared according to her instructions. Mrs. Bertram beamed, happy to be of service. In her own way she was striving to be included in the grand adventure.

"We got the airlift equipment on board, Murray,"

Harp said. "I can't wait to try it out. Suckers'll move
two tons of sand an hour."

O'Shea nodded. He caught Kate's eye and said,
"Expensive little gizmo."

"Hell, yes. But you're gonna help us out in that
department, right, Berty?"

Mrs. Bertram smiled enigmatically. Plainly she en-
joyed being courted.

"You know the risks, of course," O'Shea said. He
had opened his briefcase and was shuffling through
documents. "There's no guarantee implied."

"Murray's an old fussbudget," Harp said. "There's
gold down there. Tons of it. I can smell it. All we
gotta do is blow a few holes in the bottom."

"He's an optimist, Mrs. Bertram," O'Shea said.
He slipped on a pair of half-moon reading glasses
and fiddled with the papers. "It could take weeks.
Months."

Centuries, I thought. The next Ice Age might come
and go before the investors saw a return on their
money. Mrs. Bertram didn't seem to care. She was
caught up in the fever and she fell for the good-cop,
bad-cop routine. O'Shea was the voice of reason,
giving sound financial advice. Harper King played
the modern pirate, with his flashy confidence in
airlifts and metal detectors.

In the end the deal was sealed by a piece of jewelry.

"All this paper shuffling, it like to make us forget
the whole point of this enterprise," Harp said. He
dipped his fingers into the breast pocket of his tropical shirt. He opened his hand, flashing gold. "This
here is the point. Been buried at the bottom of the
sea for three hundred fifty years. The gold of the
Incas!" He held out the bracelet, grinning so that his
tooth was a glinting echo. "They killed for this.
Went to war, fought, died. Who knows how many
lives this piece of gold cost before it was melted

down and recast to fit the wrist of some great Renaissance lady in the court of Philip the Second."

Harp took Mrs. Bertram's hand and slipped the bracelet onto her slender, bony wrist.

"I want you to have this," he said, "now that you're a major investor."

Right after that she got out her checkbook.

I dialed Lil Cashman's number from a phone booth at Mallory Square. The night was sultry, that old tropic intimacy of sweet bougainvillea and frangipani. The pink taillights of Mrs. Bertram's limousine retreated down Whitehead Street. She was going beddy-bye at the Casa Marina, on the southside of the island, and my services as Exhibit A were no longer required.

Samantha answered.

"Hi, handsome."

"Lo, Sammie. Is your worser-half able to come to the phone?"

Her laugh tinkled in my ear. "Worser is right now about halfway to Margaritaville. The salt on the rim has her all kind of pinched-looking, you know?"

I could hear Lil in the background, demanding the phone.

"Hold your horses," Sammie said. "All I want to say to handsome is, honey, howzit going? You getting any action on *Loveboat* or what?"

"Some," I said. "Not the kind you have in mind, Sam."

"Know what? Just for the record, I don't give a damn about that ten grand. It's Lil who's all pissed off, on account of that leggy blonde snubbed her. So what I'm saying, Stash honey, is don't go feeding any more fingers to the fish on my account."

"Sure thing, Sam."

Lil came on. I could hear the booze in her voice,

the way it made her inflect every statement into a question. Margaritaville indeed. "I have bad news and good news," she said. "The bad news is named Fernando Del Ray. The good news is you don't need to go back on that boat."

"Why's that, Lil?"

"Because like Sammie said, we don't care about the money. Not when I heard about Del Ray. He's not a nice man, T.D. I talked to this attorney I know up in Broward County? She's on the Organized Crime Task Force, and the word on Del Ray is, when he doesn't like a person, that person disappears. As in never seen again?"

"Del Ray is on the lam, Lil. He skipped bail and bought himself an island in Grand Cayman, what I heard."

"A person like that, with such connections, doesn't have to be in the room to make the lights go out, okay? He's got what they call a long reach. What happened, I had a nice conversation with your friend Lieutenant Kerry, over there in his little office on Angela Street? He says, 'You talk to him, he won't listen to me.' He says you're a thick-headed conch, T.D."

"I'll take it as a compliment," I said. "What was it old Nelly wanted to tell me?"

"Same as I'm saying. Get off the boat. Your cop friend says he found out that Harper King and his pals are already under investigation by a bunch of federal agencies. The FBI, the DEA, the SEC. I can't remember if he said the CIA."

"Too many cooks," I said.

"Honey," Lil said, "I want you off, okay? I'll pay the day rate on the contract—I'll even kick in a bonus. I got you into this and now I want you out of it, *capisce*? I don't want it on my conscience, you get yourself caught in a crossfire."

"Consider yourself absolved," I said. "Say three Hail Marys and have Sammie put you to bed."

"Stash," she said, "listen to me."

I did what thickheaded conchs do when someone smart wants them to listen. I hung up.

When I got back to *Ducat*, Billy Briggs was singing. He was flat on his back on the gangway, holding his arms out to the heaven.

"Happy birthday, dear Bill-ee," he bellowed. "Happy birthday to me."

It wasn't a solo performance. Cindy Ann joined in the chorus. Billy kept trying to grab her ankles. She was sitting further up the gangway and all she had to do was kick up her heels to pull her ankles out of range. At first I didn't recognize her, on account of the clothes she had on. It was the little-girl squeak in her voice that gave it away.

"Leggo my leg!"

Billy had managed to latch on to an ankle. The result sounded like fingernails on slate.

"Leggo, honey, you hurtin' me!"

If I'd had any sense I'd have given it up, turned around, and gone back to my tin-roofed bungalow. Left Billy Briggs and Harper King and the rest of the co-conspirators to stew in the alphabet soup of government agencies. Left them for the long arm of the Del Ray organization. I was giving it serious consideration when Mindy called down from the companionway.

"Give us a hand, Stash? He doesn't want to move. all he wants to do is lie there and sing."

Mindy was trying to help Cindy Ann help Billy. Only Cindy Ann wasn't in any too good a shape herself. I managed to grab the sodden troubadour under his moist armpits and heave him to the top of the gangway. Peppermint fumes mixed with the pong of beer and sweat. Billy boy had been into the schnapps again.

"Know what?" he gasped as he toppled onto the deck. "I'm a party animal. Party *down*, bubba. Ain't that so, Cindy Ann?"

Cindy Ann had slumped down. The long platinum hair covered her face. Her purse had spilled open and Mindy was stuffing the mass of wrinkled dollar bills back into it for her.

"These two are a mess," she said. "What'll we do? Harp says we're leaving at the crack of dawn, now he's got the cash to run that airlift."

Mindy stood there with her hands on her hips. Bright, intelligent eyes, a nice, open face, and she trusted me. More than enough reason not to jump ship, if I needed a reason.

"Paul around?" I said. "Get him to give you a hand with Cindy Ann. Call a cab and take her home. I'll get party animal here into his bunk."

Billy obliged by passing out. That made him dead-weight, but at least he wasn't ruining a perfectly good song. I managed to drag him down the stairs to the cabin deck, resisting the temptation to let his head thump against the steps. I wanted Billy in one piece. He was a known quantity. He was strong and mean and he had a loathsome weakness for sweet aperitifs, but he was predictable. Or so I thought.

Naturally his cabin door was locked. I set him down and paused to catch my breath. I could hear soft music coming from Harp's suite, and the murmur of voices. Harp, Kate, and my favorite redhead, Murray O'Shea, were engaged in a spirited conversation.

Billy's keys were in his pocket. I got his door open, grabbed him by the waist of his jeans, and heaved him into his bunk. His momentum knocked the pillow aside. Under it was a nickel-plated .38.

"That's real cute, Bill," I whispered. "It's got a snub nose, just like you."

"Ugh?"

"Are we waking up, Snooghums? Say, Bill, while I've got your attention, what have you got against the new diver? You know, T.D. Stash?"

"Troublemaker," Billy muttered. "Thinks he's so smart."

"And what do you do with a troublemaker like him, Bill? Got any ideas?"

"Easy," he said thickly, never opening his eyes. "Feed 'im to the sharks."

"Maybe stick some bait in his tank rack?"

He passed out before I could get an answer, but the sneering grin on his unconscious face told it all. I should have known that a mean-tempered brute like Billy, who had bashed his best friend to death on a whim, wouldn't need much motivation to attempt murder. Being a troublemaker with a smart mouth was reason enough.

Billy was snoring as I put the pillow back over the revolver and returned his keys to his pocket. With any luck he'd assume he got into his cabin under his own steam, and that our little conversation about human sharkbait had been a dream. I eased his lock shut and crept back into the companionway.

As a rule I don't approve of carpeting on a yacht. Soaks up moisture, tends to mildew, and is generally more trouble than it's worth. In the particular, though, it has one advantage. It makes it easy to sneak up and put your ear to a cabin door. Which I did.

14

VOICES WERE being raised in the master suite. Murray O'Shea was unhappy about the way Harper King was spending money.

"Don't tell me about the bottom line," O'Shea said. "I know about the bottom line. *I'm* the bottom line, okay? Can you get that through your fat head?"

"Now, Murray," Kate said. Compared with his, her voice was a murmur. I had to strain to hear it.

"I don't get it," Harp said. He sounded puzzled, not angry. "We just got a check for two hundred large, and you're busting my chops over a lousy fifteen hundred a week?"

"Exactly my point. It's fifteen hundred that belongs in the kitty. It's fifteen hundred that's an unauthorized expense. And we agreed, all of us, there would be no unauthorized expense in this operation," O'Shea said. "I went along with the doubloons and the bracelet, big-ticket items, but I don't like you going behind my back on this one."

"What is it?" Harp said. "You want to know every little detail? What we spend on groceries? What happened, I leased those airlifts to cover our ass, okay? To make it look legit. We had a prospect of taking two hundred large off a very influential lady, I wanted us to look right. For her and for anybody who might be checking us out, see if we have the appearance of acting in a professional manner."

"Checking us out?" The way O'Shea inflected his words made me think his belligerence was at least partly induced by drink. "Who's checking us out? Give me a name."

"Hey, this is a small town. Word gets around. The locals, I get the feeling the locals are giving us the hairy eyeball."

"Do me a favor, Harp, forget the locals, okay?"

"It's just they know from salvage operations down here, Murray. This is not exactly a new idea in Key West, going after treasure in shallow water. Guys on the waterfront, these old salts, they're saying, 'He ain't even got an airlift, who's he kidding?' I was just trying to make it look legit, that's all. We *know* there are cannon down there, right? So if we use the airlift to dig a few out, Mrs. B. is going to get excited, say the right things to all her wealthy friends."

Kate said, "Harp's got a point."

"Kate, baby, you're supposed to be the level head."

I winced. Hearing O'Shea call Kate "baby" set up an internal dissonance. It made me want to twist his sunburned nose. The distraction made me lose focus on the voices for long enough to miss a new entry into the subject matter under discussion.

". . . think he wouldn't bother, considering the small scale, but he watches every penny," O'Shea was saying. "Don't forget, Freddie started out as a CPA, he knows how to read books. He's sees this lease for your new toy, he's going to want to know what is this, is Harp starting to believe his own promotions again or what? My guess, and I've known the guy since when he was starting out, he's going to say, 'Fine, Harp wants to play with this fancy equipment, it can come out of his end.' "

Harp was starting to sound less puzzled, more irritated. "Murray? You expect me to believe that this guy, who is sitting on a couple hundred million, who owns his own bank down there, who owns an island down there, you expect me to believe he gives a shit about a lousy fifteen hundred dollars? When I just promoted two hundred large and his cut is what, seventy-five percent? Murray, I just made Del Ray, correct me if I'm wrong, tonight I made him a hundred and fifty grand. And you're complaining?"

"Hey, it was nice work with the old lady. No argument. But that is a separate issue to the daily expenses, which are beginning to get out of hand. We got a fuel bill, I don't have to tell you how much 'cause you already know."

"Murray," Harp said, "do me a favor, have another drink and relax, okay? What's wrong with you is you got sick in that airplane—I don't know why you don't just *drive* down, it makes you feel that bad—you got sick and now you're taking it out on us."

The voice levels reduced to low muttering as, presumably, another dose of alcohol was administered. I was starting to get a crick in my neck. Eavesdropping is hard work. I crouched and found a thin spot in the teak door panel and waited for the conversation to heat up again.

What happened next is that someone tapped me on the shoulder. I jumped. Not high, only a foot or so. I turned, hands loose at my sides, heart thudding.

It was Mindy. She waggled her finger at me and whispered, "Naughty, naughty."

Then she smiled a secret kind of smile and walked away.

When *Ducat* finally pulled away from Mallory Wharf, it was going on ten o'clock. The "crack of dawn" had come and gone, and with it any useful direct sunlight. Cloud cover rolled in from the southeast, and stayed. I was up there on the bridge like a good little sailor, waiting for the lazybones to roll out of their bunks and get the show on the road. Using the solitary time to recheck the log entries and to think about what I'd overheard the night before. Putting it all together. Working myself up into a certain mood.

"Let's go treasure-hunting, guys. Let's spend some of Mrs. Bertram's money, or whatever is left after Fernando Del Ray takes his big cut."

I was feeling righteous. T.D. Stash, champion of the oppressed, exposer of swindlers small and large. That old fire-and-brimstone righteousness, yes, indeed, nothing touches it. A sensation not infrequently indulged by TV evangelists and attorneys general and firebrands of every persuasion. Not to mention fish-guides and unlicensed troublemakers.

Feel the good feeling, Brother Stash. Rant and rave. Let your stolid, law-abiding soul seethe with contempt for those of lesser moral fiber. Never mind about the glass houses and the zoning ordinance that proscribes rock-throwing. Get on with it. Give 'em hell.

Only thing about indulging in that righteous feeling, it tends to cloud your vision. It can fool you into confusing righteousness with being right, and before you know it, *boom*, something has snuck up and caught you from behind.

Like hurricane Celeste, for instance.

The tropical storm of that name was forming out there in the Gulf, plain to see on the NOAH radar printouts. True, the storm came into being some eight hundred miles from southern Florida. And also true that no one from NOAH or any other weather agency predicted it would turn northwest, bounce off the coast of Cuba, and slam into the Lower Keys. It just happened to happen that way.

But there is no getting around the fact that a cautious, experienced waterman like yours truly should have been on the lookout, considering the time of year. There is no getting around the fact that of all those on board the *Ducat*, I was the one who should have known better. Should have seen the warning signs, made a run for cover, saving the ship and the lives and the damnable curse of the gold coins.

Should-haves. I already had quite a collection of them. And in the course of the next few days I would collect a few more, of trophy size. I had the decks to myself for that first hour of light. Then the smell of frying bacon drew me down into the galley. Paul from Minnesota was mixing up a batch of southern-style flapjacks. I volunteered to take charge of the bacon.

"Just don't let it b-b-burn."

The stutter, as I had noticed, tended to solve itself after the first few preliminary sentences. It seemed to coincide with his feeling comfortable enough to make eye contact. I flipped the bacon, moving it away from the hot spot on the grill, and inquired as to any difficulties he and Mindy might have had taking Cindy Ann home.

"No . . . sweat," he said, taking his time to get the word out right. "The guy driving the taxi knew right where she lived. There was this roommate helped put her to bed." He fussed with the bowl of batter, adding a tablespoon of the bacon fat, and asked if I'd had any trouble getting Billy into his bunk.

"Piece of cake," I said. "He's going to have a head as big as a pumpkin, though. We better keep out of his way."

"I keep out of his way, p-p-period."

"Billy?" I said. "Now don't get spooked by Bill.

He isn't any more dangerous than a rattlesnake, or an earthquake."

Note that I didn't mention hurricane. I wasn't thinking hurricane. I wasn't thinking, period.

There was something else bothering Paul.

"Does everyone get seasick?" he wanted to know. "The first time?"

"Depends how rough it is," I said. "If it's calm you won't have any trouble. Not on a vessel as big as this."

"I've been out on the lakes back home," he said, slipping a spatula under a perfect flapjack. "This is different. You know, the ocean."

Well, I did and I didn't. But it was calm enough the first day, and most of the second, and by the time it wasn't calm so much was hitting the fan that intestinal discomfort was the least of our worries.

Mindy appeared in time for the first serving of flapjacks, wanting to know why no one had woken her. She made a point of not mentioning the comprising position she'd found me in the night before, and for that I was grateful. The only indication that she remembered was a mischievous twinkle in her eyes as she asked me to pass the syrup.

"Kate's taking Mr. O'Shea to the bus station," she said. "I knocked on Billy's door. I'm not sure, but I think he barked at me."

"He'll be wanting a raw egg," I said. "Which proves he must have a cast-iron gut."

Mindy whispered, "He's cast iron, for sure. From ear to ear."

Minnesota Paul laughed so hard he started to hiccup. By the time we anchored over the wreck site it was almost noon and he was too busy working on lunch to worry about seasickness.

Harp King uncovered the first of the bronze cannons early that afternoon. At twenty-three minutes after one, to be exact. It happened like this:

I was on the rear deck, appointed dive tender on account of my wounds, such as they were. My function was to log time on the divers in the water, have tanks ready, and make sure the airlift was functioning. The airlift equipment was what O'Shea had been bitching about, and as the afternoon wore on, I had a few complaints myself. The compressors and pumps were noisy, the discharge hoses tended to clog, and the big diesel that powered it was a cantankerous thing.

Never mind, Harp was in love. He was like a kid with a new toy. He went over the various parts with me, as proud as if he'd invented the machine, as if he really thought he might find gold with it.

"What we've got here," he said, "is a miracle of modern science. Same principle as a vacuum cleaner, only we're lifting water and sand, not air and dust. This pumps pressure through the primary hose. This is the sucker part."

The sucker part.

I thought I knew what the sucker part was. A part played alternately by Sammie, Nelson Kerry, Mrs. Bertram, and the rest of the investors. Also by T. D. Stash, who'd come pretty near to believing and who was still on board, collecting his worthless shares as much out of sheer, stubborn curiosity as in any hope of recovering Sammie's money. I assumed that was gone forever, siphoned off by Attorney O'Shea. My curiosity now centered on how Harper King planned to keep out of jail when the pyramid finally collapsed. Did he think O'Shea would do a better job of getting him off this time? Or was he going to make a run for it?

I wondered about that island Fernando Del Ray had bought. Was there room for one more rogue on that speck of Caribbean paradise?

"This here'll move five tons an hour, they tell me," Harp said, running loving hands over the coil of hoses. "That's minimum. What it takes is a strong back, strong arms, and concentration."

Spoken like a true believer. And I might have believed him, too, if I hadn't been listening outside the door to the master suite. Listening to his master's voice.

"We gonna uncover us some treasure," he said, grinning hugely. "Today's the day."

Today's the day. He'd borrowed the slogan from Mel Fisher, a real treasure-hunter who had searched for real treasure and found it, eventually. But everything I'd learned so far convinced me that Harper King was searching for nothing more original than an interesting swindle, another variation on the greatest floating crap game.

Come on, suckers, get out your checkbooks. Today's the day!

What galled me the most about the big con artist with the winning personality and the golden smile was not that he'd almost succeeded in conning me. It was that he'd saved my life. Here I was figuring how to set him up for the bust he richly deserved, and all the while a nagging voice kept whispering, "let the man go, he saved your sharkbait ass."

The salvage scheme was a fake, but the shark had been a ton of vicious reality. "It's not up to you," my little voice urged, "leave him for the SEC, the DEA, the FBI, whoever gets there first."

The object of all this internal dialogue dropped the coil of hoses over the side, shrugged on his gear, and prepared to dive on the wreck of a galleon he knew to be worthless. Before going under he spit out his mouthpiece and shouted above the thump of the idling compressors, "Wish me luck!"

Damn me, but I did. And thirty minutes later,

when Mindy surfaced with the news that he'd uncovered a bronze cannon, I was as elated as the rest of
the crew. It didn't matter that, according to Ben
Jones, the cannon came from a galleon barren of
treasure. We'd found something. Maybe Jones was
wrong. Maybe they were all wrong.

I gave Mindy a hand up to the diving platform.
She was giddy with excitement. "It's like you're
watching this film run backward," she said. "The
cannon looks like it's rising out of the bottom, only
it's really the sand being drawn off."

"You said it's bronze?"

"Has to be. No rust. A little corrosion, but not
much. Like the sand has been protecting it all these
years. Looks like maybe there's more under it."

"More cannon?"

"More *something*."

Mindy went straight back down, carrying new
tanks for Harp, who was going through a lot of air,
breathing hard as he held on to the bucking hose.
The commotion brought Billy Briggs out of his cabin,
where he'd been nursing a three-egg hangover.

"You're shitting me," he said when I told him
about the cannon. "This I gotta see."

In his hurry he didn't bother with a wet suit and
was still fastening his weight belt as he dropped
over the side. The next one up from the bottom was
Kate, who needed more film for her camera. She
seemed delighted, genuinely excited by the find.
Very convincing.

"I must admit, I had my doubts," she said, fum-
bling with wrinkled fingertips at the plexiglass camera housing. "Here, can you do this?"

As I loaded the film I wondered what she had
been doubting. Harp? The value of the airlifts? Would
raising a cannon or two really make it easier to raise
more money, find new investors? New suckers, more

like it. Or was she getting infected with the idea there might actually be something valuable waiting down there? When I handed the camera back, she placed her hand on my thigh and squeezed, thanking me. That gave me something else to think about, as the tingling shape of her fingers gradually faded.

The next time Mindy came up for fresh tanks, I suited up. I had to see what was happening down there.

"Hey," she said. "What about the stitches?"

"You just make sure there's oil in the sump of that compressor," I said, buckling the BC belt. "I'm going down for a quick peek. Be back up before my hand knows it's been underwater."

The first ten feet of water was clouded with the spew from the airlift. From there on it gradually cleared. I followed the airlift hose to the bottom. There I found Harper King, proud father of a born-again bronze cannon, at the bottom of the pit he'd created. He had anchored himself down by putting ballast stones over his fins. He was sweeping the hose back and forth with his powerful forearms, sucking away time and history, uncovering the armament of a Spanish galleon.

He'd been at it for three hours, for several tank changes. He had to be exhausted, chilled to the bone. But he wouldn't give that hose up, not to anyone, and when I finally ran out of air and headed for the shimmering surface, Harp was still down there, as happy as a kid in a brand-new sandbox.

What that did, it made me wonder.

15 _____

THAT EVENING, thanks to Billy Briggs, we had the second shark incident. We had finally dragged Harp to the surface by hauling in the airlift hose. By then the light was fading and visibility at the bottom was down to a few yards. Harp talked about rigging underwater lights, but we didn't have underwater lights.

"We'll get 'em," he vowed, accepting a beer from Kate, who was shaking her head in amused disbelief. "We'll run this job three shifts. We'll sign up, say, four more divers. Then I'll get us another airlift, we'll start punching exploratory holes in those quadrants around the cannon. We're gonna turn that sandy bottom into Swiss Cheese. Think of it!"

The curious thing was, no one wanted to leave the deck and go inside, even after the magenta sun dropped into the oily sea. It was as if the proximity of the wreck kept us there, moored to the impossible fantasy of a gold-bearing galleon lying just beneath us. I knew it was an impossible fantasy, but I was beginning to wonder if Harper King knew it or not. Could all of this jubilation about uncovering a few cannon really be faked? Or did he know something about the wreck of the reputedly worthless *Rosario* that no one else knew? Not Buster Sawyer nor Ben Jones nor any of the men who had squandered years and fortunes over her bones. Certainly not Murray

O'Shea, who clearly saw the claim site as a means to an end.

We had supper out on the rear deck, in the extended twilight of a late-August evening. Stars shone now and then through ragged, eerie holes in the cloud cover. A good sailor would have remarked on the way weather was moving high up in the atmosphere. I noticed, but it didn't make an impression. I was more interested in wolfing down the grouper Mindy had caught with a hand line tied to the rail.

"They get fish like this up in Minnesota?" I asked Paul, who was hovering over a pot of steamed cob corn, ready to dish out extras.

"We get mostly lake trout, pickerel, pike. And c-c-catfish, of course."

"C-c-catfish. Now what kind of fish is that, P-p-paul?" Billy said. His eyes registered that boozy meanness he seemed to get after only a beer or two. "What's a matter, bubba, c-c-cat got your tongue?"

I could see the boy's jaw working, but his lips remained firmly shut and he did not attempt an answer. After a while Billy quit baiting him and amused himself by jawboning a corn cob with the ferocity of a tarpon, snapping at it with his flat white teeth until the cob was denuded. Harp gave no indication of noticing any unpleasantness. He was firmly enthralled with the idea of expanding the salvage operation.

"Now, what's the intrinsic value of a bronze cannon, you might ask?" No one had, but that didn't stop Harp, who was too charged up to do more than pick at his plate of pan-fried grouper. "Say each one weighs maybe two ton. Cash value, you melted it down, maybe two thousand bucks. Hardly worth the cost of hauling it up. 'Course, it would be a sin to sell it for scrap. A sin! This is a historical artifact. We get up these cannon, prob'ly we'll locate a foundry mark, we can even pinpoint exactly where it was manufactured. That has to be worth a lot to a collector."

Kate knew exactly what the cannon were worth. "I finally got through to the radio telephone operator," she said. "Mrs. Bertram is thrilled. She said, 'I knew Harp could do it, he's got balls.' Can you believe she said that?"

But Harp was by then beyond the thrill of finding cannon or impressing his biggest investor. In his head he'd already found the real treasure, the gold itself.

"It's down there. I could *feel* it," he exulted, pacing the deck, a beer bottle untasted in his big fist. "Buried down under the cannons. I swear I must be psychic, that's how strong the feeling is. It's like I was there in a previous life or something, right there when *Rosario* hit the reef and sank. I keep seeing this vision of the cannon crashing down through the cargo hold, breaking the gold bars loose. We uncover those cannon, we'll find the gold. I know it. I feel it. I can *taste* it."

Billy, meanwhile, was up to a new trick. He had woven a big hook through the grouper head and attached a heavy line. Then he tossed the rig over the stern and tied the line to a stanchion. The next step was throwing over a bucket of grouper guts.

Mindy wanted to know what he was doing.

"Goin' for a big-game fish," he said, laughing. "Ain't that right, Stash?"

"He's fishing for shark," I said.

"Well, it sure ain't *fly* fishing, Mr. Fish Guide. No way. Ain't no eight-pound test line. We gonna hook us a big mother, have us some fun."

Chumming at night in these waters is almost certain to attract sharks. The delectable bait of the grouper head virtually guaranteed a strike. When the line tightened, indicating a hit, Billy got out on the dive platform and hauled in a medium-sized lemon shark. He got a gaff into its tail and hauled it up backward onto the grate, where he clubbed it to death with a length of iron pipe.

"Can you eat that thing?" Harp wanted to know. He was leaning on the rail, watching his divemaster butcher the six-foot shark.

"*You* can, you want," Billy said. His forearms were slick with blood as he chopped into the fish with his dive knife. "I ain't eatin' no shark, bubba. Shark is nigger food, ain't fit for no white man. 'Course, a shark, now, it likes nothing better than to eat one of its own."

Harp had switched on the stern lights. The lights and the shark guts had attracted some hungry cousins of the butchered lemon. I saw blacktips, a small tiger, and more of the lemons, all of them snapping at the chunks Billy heaved from the platform. The sea ran up through the grates, soaking him to the knees, but Billy was into killing like Harp was into finding gold. He didn't care about getting wet or risking his bare feet in seas that were soon boiling with shark.

Beside me, Mindy whispered, "You know what? He's crazy."

"Guys like Bill, they tend to erode species loyalty," I said. "Makes you want to root for the fish."

She laughed. It was a nervous kind of laugh. No wonder. Watching Billy Briggs knee-deep in snapping sharks would make any normal person nervous.

"Jaws!" he shouted, cackling. "Jaws, where is you? Is you out there, Jaws? Come and get it!"

Determined to keep this attentive audience, he rigged a monster hook in the shark head and heaved it out as far as he could. Jerking the line, he pulled it out of the gaping mouths of the smaller sharks until a big tiger lunged out of the deep and snatched it, immediately heading for the bottom.

"Oh, baby," Billy said, paying out line. "Oh, did you see the size of that mother?"

He threw out the line, letting the tiger run. When he thought it safe to set the hook, he quickly looped the line around a cleat. The line tightened and began to vibrate.

"Come on, Harp!" Billy shouted. "Get down there and help me haul this mother in. Come on, bubba, we got a thousand pounds of tiger shark, and it ain't by the tail, neither!"

Whatever Harper King was, he wasn't the kind of man who could resist a dare. He clambered over the side before Kate could stop him. Slipping and sliding on the blood-drenched dive platform. Nor did he hesitate to plunge his hands into the water and take hold of the vibrating line.

"You heave," Billy ordered. "I'll loop off the slack."

That was how they did it. Hauled in that big tiger a yard at a time. Harp pulling, heels dug into the grate, and Billy cleating line as it came.

Paul from Minnesota gaped at the scene. Not two hours before, a twenty-pound grouper had been the biggest fish he'd ever seen. Now, rolling and plunging a scant thirty yards astern, was a half a ton of shark. A very pissed-off shark.

"Is this d-d-dangerous?" the boy wanted to know. He was clinging to the cap rail, making damn sure he wouldn't slip into the teeming sea.

"Dangerous enough," I said. "If the line breaks, say, and snags around your wrist or your ankle."

Kate heard that and ordered Harp to get his dumb ass back on the deck. He ignored her. He was into it, man against beast. Giving in to the primal urge. Purging the fear in a rush of adrenaline.

"Come to papa," Harp crooned. "Bring it on home, Sweetie Pie."

The big tiger seemed to be tiring. You could see where the heavy line had cut deeply into its jaw and where the dark point of the monster hook was firmly embedded in the bone. Sweetie Pie kept snapping. Maybe its dim brain had enough intelligence to comprehend that the only chance of survival was to sever the line. The jaws snapped as it rolled, turning the water to spume. Its flat eyes were strangely inanimate; indeed, they seemed painted on.

"It doesn't look real," Mindy said.

The thing about sharks is, they *don't* look quite real. Aeons of evolution have produced a perfect mechanical carnivore, a thing that exists only to feed continuously. So long as the shark lives, its sturdy coat of skin looks more like airbrushed plastic than mortal flesh. Its whipsaw movements seem programmed. The snapping jaws appear to be manipulated by mechanical springs. The eyes have less life than a chip of smoked glass. Only the ragged rows of teeth are imperfect enough to look real.

Sweetie Pie, as Harp christened the tiger, had plenty of teeth. As they slowly winched the beast up to the dive platform, it became even more agitated, snapping its great jaws, tossing its blunt snout like a dog trying to shake free of a leash. It became clear that it was not going to break free, that the monster hook was just too deeply embedded to be shrugged off, no matter how it struggled.

When they had it cleated tight to the platform, Billy took up the pipe and started beating it on the head. This had no effect and in one snapping lunge the shark seized the pipe and began to maul it. Billy didn't like that, not one bit.

"Time to say bye-bye, Sweetie Pie!"

He must have had the .38 in the rear pocket of his jeans, because the next thing I knew he was pressing the muzzle to Sweetie Pie's head and firing. The frenzied cousins, reacting to the death tremors of the big tiger, began to bite at its fins. The water boiled as they tore into the unprotected underbelly.

Billy had the empty pistol in his hand as he came up over the rail.

"You see that mother die?" he wanted to know. "You all see it die?"

Harp had seen it. When he hoisted himself back on deck it was plain his mood of exuberance had been diluted. He liked the catching part, the fight. The killing left him cold.

"We better make an early night of it," he said, hitching an arm around Kate and pulling her close. "Tomorrow's gonna be the day. I can feel it in my bones."

Below, still lashed to the dive platform, the rapidly diminished body of the tiger trembled with the ferocity of the feeding. Billy Briggs, spattered with blood and viscera, strutted under the lights, his eyes as flat and empty as the shark's.

"He scares me," Mindy said.

We were in my cabin. Mindy was sitting on the bunk, chin resting on her knees. Close enough so I could smell her natural perfume and see the flecks of gold in her eyes. Close enough so I wanted to touch her, but didn't. There had been no invitation—she had not come for physical comfort, I assumed, but to voice what troubled her about the situation on board *Ducat.*

So I sat on my hands.

"Billy's mean," I said. "But he's dumb."

"I didn't mean Billy. Not that he isn't scary sometimes. I meant the little guy from Miami. The lawyer."

"O'Shea? Why, did he try to put moves on you?"

Mindy shook her head. Her dark bangs were starting to lighten at the ends into a chestnut glow that matched her deep tan. "I can't explain it. Something about the guy gives me the creeps, you know? Just the way he looks at me. Like he comes from a different planet or something."

"It's that funny little mustache," I said.

She ignored the joke. "It's just, I got the impression he was trying to pull a fast one."

"He's a lawyer," I said. "They tend to give that impression. It doesn't necessarily mean they're crooked. Only sometimes."

Mindy smiled faintly. "Do me a favor, T.D.? Don't treat me like I'm some dumb little chick?"

"Oops," I said, and proceeded to apologize. I agreed there was something "off" about Murray O'Shea, attorney at law. What I couldn't explain, without getting into more hot water, was that treating her like a kid sister was my way of diffusing the sexual attraction.

"O'Shea is certainly a slippery character," I said. "He rubs me the wrong way, too. Which is why I wanted to hear what he had to say. You know, when you snuck up on me last night, outside the master suite."

She chuckled, shaking her head. "I wasn't sneaking up. Anyhow, I didn't mean to be. Was that what you were doing, checking out O'Shea? I thought, I guess I assumed it was something to do with Kate. You know, fooling around with her. Or something."

"I'd sooner fool with a bucket of blasting caps."

"You don't think she's sexy?"

"I didn't say that," I said. "I thought you were worried about O'Shea, not what I may or may not think about Kate Starling."

"Well," she said, her eyes sparkling, "I was kind of thinking maybe it went together somehow. Murray and Kate. Like they had something going. Not a sex thing. Something else."

I asked her to be specific. She said she couldn't, that it was only a feeling.

"Just there was these little flashes between them, when they thought no one was noticing. Like, you know, messages. Like they both thought Harp was a little goofy and they had to humor him. You notice anything like that?"

"I guess so," I said. "Maybe."

If I had it to do over again, I'd tell her right then everything I knew about what was really going on aboard *Ducat*. Trouble is, you never have it to do over again. You have to live with how you played it the first time through. There's one thing I don't regret, though, and that's what happened next.

Mindy leaned forward. "You can kiss me," she said. "If you want, you can pretend I'm Kate Starling."

"What I'll pretend," I said, "I'll pretend it's you."

It seemed like the right thing to do. Soon enough it didn't have anything to do with right or wrong, or pretending. There was no thinking or planning or reasoning, only touching and being touched, kissing and being kissed. And Mindy slipping out of her clothes and guiding me into her heat, into the eager, surging hips and the lingering pleasure of each deliberate caress.

I was floating in that pleasant half-world between satiation and sleep when Mindy said, "Know what? It's about time for the postcoital confessions."

I said, "Huh?"

She said, "I'll tell you mine if you'll tell me yours."

There was something in the tone of her voice that woke me all the way up.

"What are we talking about?" I asked.

"Job descriptions," she said. "Yours is listed as 'Unlicensed Operative.' "

"You've lost me."

"Okay," she said. "I'll go first."

What Mindy had previously told me about herself had been based, in part, she said, on the truth. For instance, it was true she had left Elk Rapids, Michigan, and moved in with her sister in Sarasota. What she had neglected to mention was a two-year stint at a junior college, majoring in jurisprudence, with a minor in criminology. After graduation she'd aced the Civil Service exams and gone to work as an investigator.

I sat up, bumping my head on the bunk rack. "Ouch," I said. "You mean you're undercover? What outfit? FBI? DEA?"

"Don't laugh," she said. "The SEC."

"Securities and Exchange? They've got undercover agents? Since when?"

"It's a new program," she said. "The idea is we're supposed to recover diverted securities, that way the project funds itself. When I first got hired it was for the Felony Investigation Unit, which in the SEC means reading documents, basically. Playing with the software, checking the books. Boring stuff. So when this new program got implemented, I jumped at it."

"New program?"

"You know, the Del Ray investigation."

A lot of it I already knew. The multi-million-dollar securities swindle engineered by Fernando Del Ray and his associates had set off alarms in most of the federal and state agencies. The recovery of diverted funds was a high priority at the SEC offices. With Del Ray out of the country and unlikely to return voluntarily, the lines of investigation had begun to concentrate on the associates like Attorney O'Shea and former employees Harper King and Kate Starling.

"That's where I came in," Mindy said. "The theory is that O'Shea is laundering funds, somehow transferring Del Ray holdings to the Cayman Island accounts before we can nail the stuff in court."

"And you think King-Ducat Salvors is part of the laundry?"

"That's the theory. So far I haven't found anything that would hold up in court."

"How'd you get on to me?"

"Routine," she said. "When Billy signed you up, I had them plug your name into the computer. You're on file with the DEA, did you know that? Listed under 'Unlicensed Operative.' "

"Sure," I said. "I cover the waterfront."

"Don't look so smug. It's a very small file. So come on, T.D., tell me who you're working for."

"Who wants to know?"

"Me. Well, me and my boss. He's a guy, my boss, he wants to fill in all the blanks."

"I can only give you name, rank, and serial number."

"It's Mrs. Bertram, right?"

"Wrong," I said. "I'm working for a lawyer who is representing one of the small investors. It doesn't matter who. Satisfied?"

Mindy gave me a sleepy grin and slipped back into my arms.

"Not quite," she said.

16 _____

IT WAS Mindy who found the first coin. Partly that was on account of the problem with the sharks. The commotion over who could eat the most of Sweetie Pie attracted about every shark for miles around. They came in all sizes and varieties: makos, hammers, dogfish, lemons, blacktips, and tigers. At dawn the whole crowd was still there, ranging around the stern, rubbing up under the dive platform and generally causing a nuisance.

"They're your friends," I said to Billy. "Tell 'em to go home."

"I ain't scared of no sharks."

"I wish I was as tough as you, Bill," I said. "If I was as tough as you, I'd have myself mounted and hung on a wall."

He scowled. "What's that supposed to mean?"

"Means I've got a big mouth."

He laughed. "I could a tole you that. Fact is, bubba, them sharks got full bellies. They won't harm us none. That hammerhead went after you, he was the exception to the rule."

I noticed how he avoided meeting my eyes when he said that. Did he remember mumbling about his nasty trick with the baitfish that night I dragged him into his cabin to sleep off a schnapps overdose? I still didn't know exactly why he'd tried to turn me into a shark snack, but I was beginning to think it was nothing more complicated than that Billy got a kick out of watching things die.

Which made it all the more important that he not tumble to the fact that Mindy was working under-cover, gathering evidence that might well send him back to jail.

"I think what we should do," I said. "We'll go over the bow, follow the anchor rode down."

Harp concurred. He shared my lack of enthusiasm for entering shark-infested waters. Kate, complain-ing of an ear infection, elected herself dive-tender. She took charge of the compressors with her usual flair of competence. You got the impression if the finicky diesel misbehaved it would be in big trouble with Kate.

The air in that reddest of red dawns had a quality of hot, oppressive heaviness that made breathing seem an effort. Strange weather, even for August. I was looking forward to getting into the water and filling my lungs with the cool, regulated air. Before squirming into my wet suit, I loaded the bang stick Harp had given me. It came with a cleaning kit and six cartridges. You got only one shot before it re-quired reloading, so the idea was to make it good. A killing shot.

"You sure your hand is okay?" Mindy wanted to know.

She wasn't worrying about my hand, which was healing nicely. She was wondering if my having been spooked by the hammerhead attack would af-fect my dive safety. We both knew panic was the single biggest danger, that it killed a lot more divers than that rarity, a mortal shark attack.

"I'm fine," I said.

And I was. My confidence wasn't a macho reac-tion, the get-back-on-your-horse syndrome. It was based on knowing why the hammerhead had picked on me, because of the bait jammed in my tank rack. Knowing I'd been set up for the attack, I was determined not to let it happen again. Just prior to the dive I went over my equipment with great care. I disassembled the regulator, checked on the springs and valve, did the drill with my BC vest, weight belt release, mask plate, even my wrist compass. Then I made Mindy do the same with her gear. All part of making sure Billy wasn't trying a new variation on his old trick.

Harp kept trying to hurry us. "Come on, sport. We got cannons to the left of us, cannons to the right. And treasure underneath."

As it happened the treasure wasn't underneath the cannons. It wasn't anywhere near them, or even close to the wreck of the *Rosario*. It wasn't Spanish treasure at all.

The idea was, we'd follow the anchor chain to the bottom, then double back to the wreck site—avoiding, we hoped, the swarm of sharks. We saw barracuda, big ones, and a few dogfish, but no sharks of worrisome size. Mindy led the way. Her lithe young body was full of energy. I had a pretty good idea just how much energy that particular body was capable of expressing, and it was all I could do to keep up.

At the bottom we counted heads: Harp, Billy, Mindy, and yours truly. Billy pointed out the compass course to follow. Once more Mindy swam in the lead.

I followed the flash of her white power fins, enjoying the serene coolness of the water. Basking, as I swam, in the afterglow of the lovemaking that had lasted until the wee hours. Lovemaking that had, in the pure physical intensity of passion, blurred any distinction in our respective roles aboard *Ducat*. With Mindy all the lights had come on, all the bells had rung. It was, I sensed, the real thing, the genuine article. I didn't feel protective toward her, exactly, but I did feel a strong urge to deepen the relationship somehow, to touch again on equal terms and in a time and place where we would not be distracted by the necessity of subterfuge.

How that might be accomplished was what I was pondering when her white fins vanished.

My first reaction was *shark*. I grabbed the bang stick and twisted around. My second reaction was profound relief. Mindy was there. She had gone off on a tangent, abandoning the compass course, but she was there. I followed, keeping the bang stick at the ready.

Just in case.

When I got to her, Mindy was hovering over a hummock of mud that jutted up from the gravel bottom. Bubbles streamed through her hair, wreathing her in a halo of silver light. Her buoyance was a little off and she was holding herself in place by grabbing at the roots of the seaweed growing on the hummock of mud. Or that's what it looked like, at first.

What the hell? I thought.

Then I saw the glowing yellow eyes. A myriad of them scattered over the hummock, peeking through the seaweed. Bright, blinking golden things. Mindy had one in her free hand and she held it out for me to see.

A coin.

A gold coin.

A big fat gold coin.

There were more gold coins scattered over the hummock, buried in the swaying seaweed. Lots of them. Dozens and dozens. Hundreds. More than I could count. Suddenly, from out of nowhere, a hand shot under me, dislodging some of the mud. More coins appeared.

Harp King shook a coin-filled fist in my faceplate. He was rolling his eyes, waggling his eyebrows. Honking on his respirator. Delirious with silent joy.

GOLD.

Billy Briggs got into the act. He did the sensible thing, which was to place marker buoys around the hummock and inflate them. Then he came in with his knife and started digging into the mud, dislodging clusters of coins. We grabbed, scooped, gathered them in. We filled Mindy's net bag, then mine.

We hyperventilated, all of us, getting high on oxygen and the thrill of finding gold. When the small net bags were full of coins, Harp unhooked his tank and wiggled out of his neoprene dive pants like a walrus peeling off the top layer of blubber. He tied off the legs and we filled his rubber britches with handful after handful of coins. Going happily nuts. Laughing around our mouthpieces, wasting air.

Air didn't matter. What mattered was gold. The stuff of wonder and magic. Handling it was intoxicating. It made me love everyone. Not only Mindy, but Harper King, too. The big, phony goof—he'd found it! The treasure was real! King-Ducat Salvors was no longer a swindle, even if it had started out that way.

The thrill of the gold washed everything else away. The rapture filled me. I even loved Billy Briggs. Well, not quite. I loved the way he dug furiously into the mud hummock, knife flashing, spilling coins into my waiting hands. You *had* to love that.

There was no way to carry the gold-stuffed dive pants to the surface. Far too heavy. We didn't think of that until we tried to lift the thing. By then we were running out of air, all of us, sucking hard on

the respirators and grinning at one another. Four
stooges, befuddled by heavy metal.

It was Harp who jerked his thumb up. Harp who
came to his senses. We had to surface or drown.
Mindy carried one of the small coin bags, I the
other. Holding on for dear life as we kicked for the
surface, fighting against the weight. Finally, my foggy
brain remembered the design function of the buoyancy vest. I inflated mine, and Mindy followed suit.

When we popped to the surface, *Ducat* was anchored two hundred yards away. It was a long hard
kick, carrying that kind of weight. We were almost
to the transom before I sobered up enough to notice
we were swimming through seas thick with circling
fins.

We were on deck, spilling out the net bags, when
Mindy remarked on the half-moon bite in Harp's left
power fin.

He laughed at it.

"Could have taken my leg off at the knee, I
wouldn't have noticed. Hey, Kate, honey, will you
take a look at this?"

Harp poured coins from hand to hand. If his grin
was any wider he'd have split down the middle.
Kate was looking. No problem there. Her expression
was a mixture of disbelief and puzzlement. Right
away she noticed what was wrong.

"Those are twenty-dollar gold pieces," she said.
"Not Spanish doubloons."

"There's more where these came from," Harp
crowed. "A whole pants load. Thousands more. We
got to rig up some kind of bucket retrieval."

"Look at the date," Kate insisted. "Look at the
date!"

I wiped the salt from my eyes and looked. It took

a few beats for dawn to break through the gold-induced blur.

"1849," I said. "They're stamped 1849. Hell, these are U.S. Mint. They're United States of America."

Kate started laughing. She laughed until the tears streamed down her cheeks. Shaking her head and laughing at the dumb luck of it all.

Harp put a gold piece in his mouth and clowned, making a face. Then he spit the coin out and said, "We hit the jackpot, honey. Makes no matter it's the wrong jackpot. What counts is we found it. You know what? I'm gonna make old Murray eat a bellyful of this gold. We'll pound it out flat, like his goddamn veal."

Billy had very little to say. He immediately started rigging a bucket retrieval system. Theories about the origins of the coins were apparently of no interest to him. A Civil War gunboat (Mindy's idea), a U.S. Mint shipment to Cuba (Harp's), an act of piracy interrupted by a storm (mine), who cared where the gold had come from, or what nineteenth-century ship had wrecked itself on the same stretch of reef as the *Rosario*? That was idle speculation. What mattered to Billy—and what he thought should matter to all of us—was getting back down there and bringing it back up.

His single-mindedness was infectious. We stopped the scuttlebutt and got back to work. While Harp and Mindy rerigged the airlift, I lowered the chase boat from the davits and anchored it directly over the spot where the coins had been disgorged from the bottom. Visibility was such that I could just make out the circle of buoys Billy had set out.

Paul, who had emerged batter-splattered from the galley to join the celebration, was drafted to help man the smaller boat. His job was to run the winch system Billy had assembled, pulling the retrieval baskets to the surface.

Before we began the second and final dive, Billy excused himself. To use the head, he said, ducking inside. I was too excited about the sudden reversal in fortune to pay much attention to what Billy was doing. It was only later, after it all started coming apart, that I realized he must have slipped up to the bridge and used the ship-to-shore telephone to contact O'Shea.

It was only one of the mistakes I would make that day.

We worked like demons as long as the light lasted. All of the coins that would be recovered were found within the first three feet of the gravel bottom, in an area not much bigger than an average dining room. We uncovered four massive bronze hasps, badly corroded, and a few thin slats of what might have been cedar. The hasps, Harp surmised, had once been used to seal iron chests or lockers. Maybe the cedar slats had been used to separate layers of coins. We never knew for sure.

Nor did we find a wreck. Harp and Billy and I traded off on the airlift, blasting a hole that, by the time the sun had set, had hit bedrock and spread out to a circumference of more than fifty feet. It was a damned big hole and it yielded nothing but rocks. Big rocks, medium rocks, small rocks, pebbles. No timbers, no wreckage, nothing to indicate the vessel that must be transporting a shipment of newly minted gold pieces.

When it was too dark to see the end of the hose, we wearily surfaced. The sharks, either bored or more probably put off by the discharge from the airlift, had departed. The other thing I noticed, hauling myself up on the dive platform, were the sets of swells marching in from the southeast.

"That's weird," I said.

"What's weird?" Billy, clearly, thought *I* was.

"There's no wind. We've got a ten-foot swell and no wind."

"So?" he said. "Be grateful."

The sunset was blood-orange. The black clouds along the horizon were as thin as a knife cut. The heavy air was stale and charged with ozone.

"Harp, know what?" I said. "Maybe what we better do, up anchor and get the hell in."

He stopped peeling off his wet-suit top and gave me a look that made me feel like I'd just emerged from an alien spacecraft.

"The first rule," he said, "according to salvage practice we are obliged to maintain a presence on the claim site. We fail to maintain presence, anyone comes along can take what they find."

"Take a look at that sky," I said.

"Yeah," he said. "Very pretty. Hey, Billy, we got a set of scales around here?"

I didn't press the point about the disintegrating sky. What the hell, I thought, when the bad weather arrived we could fire up the engines and make a run for it. After all, we were only thirty miles from Key West and *Ducat* had the size and heft to ride out a squall.

Also, like everyone else I was virtually interested in seeing how much gold we'd recovered.

We weighed the stuff on a set of a hand-held fish scales, since the scale pan could only accommodate about forty pounds at a time. After each portion of the treasure was weighed we loaded the gold pieces into plastic fish boxes. Five of them, finally. When all the coins were heaped in the boxes Kate punched the total button on her calculator and announced that we had five hundred and sixty-three pounds.

Or roughly nine thousand ounces.

Or about three and a half million dollars at melt-down rates.

Not counting what the antique coins might be worth to collectors. Certainly more than the spot-market price. Already we knew about spot-market prices. Eight hours of handling the stuff had made instant experts of everyone involved. We began to talk knowingly of assayer's fees, handling charges, the bite Uncle Sam would demand.

"The feds will try to put the whole shebang in escrow," I said, recalling the troubles Mel Fisher had had with various state and federal agencies.

Harp's cupped hands were heavy with coin. "The bastards," he said. "We found the stuff. It's ours. Screw the IRS."

The sentiment was warmly received. We had the goodies and the first impulse was to hoard. Find yourself a cave and bury your share. Thumb your nose at tax collectors. Or the other shareholders, for that matter. What had the Mrs. Bertrams done, other than provide paper money? They hadn't braved the shark-frothed seas. They hadn't hovered at the bottom of the Gulf, or dug gold from the mud with their bare hands.

It was ours. It was mine. The gold was me me me.

"The beauty of it," Harp said, letting coins slip through his blunt fingers and jangle back into the fish boxes. "The beauty of it is, there's more where this came from. This is just an indicator. Under the *Rosario* cannons, that's where the real motherlode is. Tons of it. A couple of hundred million, that's what's down there. *Real* money."

Like three million wasn't real money. Already King had set his sights up a few notches to superwealth, the motherlode. He was like a junkie needing a bigger boost to keep the high. A thrill worth having was a thrill worth repeating. He got no argument from the crew of *Ducat*. We were too busy, all of us, recalculating the par value of our shares.

"Tell you what, Paul," Harp said. "I'm prepared to make a trade. A gold piece for every bottle of champagne you can find."

"You bet! Let's party," the boy said. The prospect of reward had removed any impediment to his speech.

He went off at a run, heading for the galley. It was right about then, with champagne on the way, that I heard the mosquito whine of an approaching speed-boat.

17 ─────────────────────────────────

MURRAY O'SHEA was the color of money.
Green money. He was crouching in the padded cockpit of a Cigarette racer as it maneuvered
under *Ducat*'s boarding ladder. Judging from the
look on Harp's face, the sudden arrival had taken
him by surprise.

"Son of a bitch," Harp said under his breath.
"Look what the cat drug in. Kate, honey, you by
any chance put in a call to old Murray?"

"No," Kate said, casting a venomous glance at
Billy Briggs, who was throwing down a line to the
driver of the Cigarette. "Why would I do a thing like
that?"

Billy lowered the ladder. The swell was running
pretty good and O'Shea had to time his grab at the
lower rungs as the smaller boat bumped against
Ducat's big hull. The man at the controls of the
Cigarette stepped away from the console and helped
the lawyer get his feet braced. The mate, a big,
broad-shouldered hulk of a man, jammed rubber
bumpers between the two hulls. While O'Shea staggered up the boarding ladder, Billy rigged spring
lines to the hot-looking racer. I caught a glimpse of
the name of the transom. *Hideaway*.

"Murray, you old sun of a gun," Harp said, em-
bracing the smaller man. "I guess good news travels
fast, huh?"

"I hate boats," O'Shea said. "I hate water. I hate the waves on the water. Is it on the level, Harp? You made a hit?"

"See for yourself."

There was something in the lawyer's face that made me uneasy, and it wasn't just his greenish complexion. Maybe it was the way his eyes shifted from Harper King to the gold. The way a patriot's eyes will shift to the flag. No pledge of allegiance was necessary, it was obvious that O'Shea's loyalty lay with the heap of coins at his feet.

The little man knelt next to one of the plastic fish boxes and stroked his fingertips over the pile of gold inside. Like he expected the treasure to arch its back and purr. His complexion began to improve. Touching the gold seemed to cure his seasickness.

"Here you go, Mr. King. I got a whole case. Twelve bottles."

"Set it down, Paul. Maybe Murray and his friends will join us for a drink. That what they'd like, Murr, a glass of champagne?"

"What " O'Shea sounded slightly stunned, as if fingering the coins had drugged him.

"Those two gorillas. 'Scuze me, your legal assistants, whatever they are. The sharp dresser is, I believe, Teddy. The other one, the big guy, I may have met him once. His name is . . .?"

"This is Boone," O'Shea said.

Boone looked like he might have had a Seminole grampa somewhere in the family tree. He wore a baggy white guayabera that bloused full over his waist. He had on chinos and clean white sneakers. He kept his hands loose at his sides, nodding slightly when his name was pronounced.

"Right. How could I forget?" There was an edge to Harp's voice I'd never heard before. A grating tone of submerged anger. "So, hey, Boone, Teddy, you want a drink, or what?"

Teddy was, as Harp had mentioned, a sharp dresser. He had looked perfect driving the flashy Cigarette racer, with his lose cotton slacks, the boat shoes with no socks, unbuttoned silk shirt, and his health-spa tan. He had his hands in the pockets of a thin leather windbreaker. The tips of his teeth showed where he was pretending to smile.

Harp was popping champagne corks, passing out the foaming bottles. Boone and Teddy both declined. The latter kept his hands in his jacket pockets. Murray tried to break the mood by clinking his bottle against the bottle Kate was holding.

"So," he said, "you did it."

To someone not paying attention, the scene might have appeared to be copacetic. O'Shea was smiling. Kate was smiling. Billy had a bottle in each fist and he was grinning, too. There were so many teeth showing it looked like a convention of Miami dentists.

What was wrong with the picture were the two gents known as Boone and Teddy. They had declined champagne. They did not speak. Teddy, the smaller one with the sharp clothes, was doing something with his mouth that might be described as smiling, but it wasn't the real thing. The big guy, Boone, was utterly impassive. The champagne, the gold, the fancy boats—none of it touched him.

Harp shook up a bottle and sprayed it playfully at the lawyer.

"So, hey, Murr," he said, "who was it, a little bird told you? No, I get it, you're psychic. You saw it all in your crystal ball."

O'Shea wiped the flecks of foam from his face. His smile was tight enough to squeak. "We just happened to drop by," he said. "We were in the neighborhood."

"Golly," Harp said. "What a coincidence, you happened to be in the neighborhood. The Cigarette boat,

Murray, it's got real class. You borrow it from Freddie Del Ray by any chance?"

"He's a generous man, Mr. Del Ray."

"You gotta like it, 'Fernando's Hideway.' I'd whistle a few bars, but I can't quite remember how it goes. Dum-dee-doo-doo, something like that, right, Murray?"

Billy had found the bottom of one of his bottles. His eyes were starting to get that hard, mean glint. "Hey, Murray," he said, "how about we get this show on the road? There's a line of squalls going to hit us in about twenty minutes. See that sky over there?"

Harp laughed. He shook the bottle and squirted foam at Billy, who ducked away, feinting like a boxer. "Come on, Billy. You afraid of a little wet weather? You gonna melt? You want, I'll hold your umbrella."

Murray O'Shea dropped his bottle over the side, as casually as if he was setting it down on a table. "Harp? Listen to me. You're getting worked up over nothing, okay?" he said. "Myself and these two gentlemen, we're only here to help. We came out here to offer protection. Think of us, Harp, try thinking like we're an insurance policy. A deterrence, in case any of the local bandidos get wise, try to take you off."

"Murray?" Billy said, interrupting. "I ain't kidding about them squalls. Jesus, look at the white caps over there."

There was bad news on the way, Billy was right about that. The clouds rushed like smoke along the dark horizon, over a sea turning rapidly white. Maybe five miles away and coming fast. At the moment, though, Harper King was the center of attention and he wasn't about to give up the stage.

"You and Terrible Ted, you're here to help out, is that it?" he said. "I heard Teddy called all kinds of names, I never heard him called a 'deterrence.' That's a new one. Tell you what, Ted, you're here out of the goodness of your heart. Why don't you take your hands out of your pockets, have a drink with your old buddy Harp?"

Ted did not respond. He had an inner stillness that was even more intimidating than the weapon he obviously had in the jacket pocket. Once or twice before I'd bumped into individuals with that kind of rare physical presence. It was never fun. It was always dangerous.

"I get it," Harp said. "Teddy's not talking because you're his mouthpiece, Murray. You got him off that time, now he owes you."

"Ted has his own methods of expression," O'Shea said. "As you know."

Billy said, "Hey, Murray?"

"Yeah, yeah. You're predicting rain."

"Not just rain. Feel that air starting to move? Them squalls are coming like a motherfucker, Murray. We better get inside."

"How about it, Harp?" O'Shea said. "Care to move your party inside?"

"Why don't we ask Terrible Ted? Whatta ya say, Ted, you want us inside? Did you see that, Murray? Teddy nodded. So I guess we better pick up your toys and go inside."

The gold. That snapped everybody into action. Even the implacable Boone lent a hand, shoving the fish boxes into the companionway. The last box was safe inside when the front arrived. The rain hit with stinging force, accompanied by a high-pitched humming in *Ducat's* rigging.

It was an effort, shoving the companionway door shut against the wind. I said, "That's not your regular mail-order squall."

"Tell me about it," Billy said.

Ducat was moving, swinging around to face the

wind. The bow lifted, tugging against the anchor chain.

O'Shea said, "What's wrong with the boat? Why are we moving?"

Billy explained about the wind and the anchor.

"Great," O'Shea said. "Wonderful. Boone, do you have those pills?"

Boone reached into the guayabera, extracting a small bottle. Dramamine. He gave the bottle to O'Shea, whose hands were trembling slightly.

"I hate everything about the ocean," he said. "I even hate the sea gulls."

"Hey, Ted," Harp said. His shirt was soaked, clinging to his big chest. "Hey, Teddy, okay if we all go into the salon, keep up this congenial atmosphere?"

Ted shrugged. "You're the captain," he said.

"Whoa! He speaks. Hey, Murray, Terrible Ted has spoken."

The crystal chandelier in the main salon was shivering. Harp looked out into the darkness beyond the row of blurry portholes. When he turned, the gentle smile was back on his face. "Whatta ya think, boys, some squall, huh? This blows through, we better head back to Key West pronto."

O'Shea dropped uneasily into a chair, almost missing it as the deck shifted under his feet. "I *hate* this," he said.

Kate said, "Where's Boone?"

"He'll be right back," Billy said.

"That wasn't the question, Billy," Harp said. "The question was, where'd he go?"

Billy laughed. "Big ape like Boone, he goes wherever he wants."

Boone was gone about five minutes. I thought about following him, but Teddy stationed himself by the door and I wasn't ready to find out what he had in his jacket pocket. Not just yet.

Mindy, uncharacteristically silent, went to the stereo and put on a tape. A bass guitar thumped through
the speakers, followed by a splash of cymbals. She
slipped her arms around my waist.

"Give me a hand," she said. "We'll mix some
drinks."

Ted watched us move to the bar. Boone returned.
He nodded at O'Shea, who was gripping the arms of
his chair, his expression rigid.

Mindy opened a bottle of Scotch. "I think we're in
big trouble," she said in a husky whisper. I had to
concentrate to hear her above the high pitch of the
wind.

"I know," I said. "This is no regular squall."

"Not the weather," she said, maintaining a frozen
smile as she poured the whiskey. "Those two creeps.
The one called Ted was up for a murder charge in
Lauderdale. He's a contract killer."

Mindy had a funny gleam in her eye. It seemed
everyone was getting a gleam off that gold. It made
me want to find a mirror and see if I was suffering
from the same look.

"Wait a second," I said. "How do you know that?"

"There isn't time to go into that now. I know what
I'm talking about, you've got to believe me."

"Okay," I said. "I do."

And I did. What to do about it was another matter. The more immediate problem of the worsening
storm became apparent as *Ducat* lurched suddenly.
The deck tipped downward. I landed on my knees,
spilling Scotch all over the carpet. Books flew out of
the bookcase, striking the bulkhead and falling to
the deck like broken-winged birds.

When he got his breath back O'Shea screamed.
"Jesus! What the hell was *that*?"

Ted was braced against the door frame. His hands
were finally out of his jacket pockets. The butt of an
automatic pistol protruded from the elastic waist of

his designer pants. Boone was sitting on the deck, legs spread. His mouth was open. For some reason I was surprised to see that he had a small pink tongue.

"Fucking anchor come loose," Billy said. He didn't sound happy. Adrenaline had chased the champagne from his head. "That's what it felt like. Like it come loose, then caught again."

That was exactly what it felt like. I had to admire Billy's seamanship. Harp, for some reason, looked happy. Like the storm was his idea. Like he wanted credit for what was going on out there.

"You okay, Murray?" he said. "You're looking a little green around the gills, partner. You got any objections, we fire up the engines and head for home?"

O'Shea had no objections. Whatever game he had in mind that required players like Teddy and Boone, it would clearly have to wait.

The climb up to the bridge was an adventure. Each time *Ducat* came up short on the anchor rode, her swaying motion would suddenly shift violently. When Boone slipped going up the ladder, his guayabera rode up high enough to reveal that he, too, had a pistol jammed in his belt.

Harp, leading the way, was defiantly cheerful. As the yacht dipped and bucked, he bellowed, "Take your Dramamine, boys! Ain't we got fun?"

The fun was just beginning. The bridge was as black as midnight. The big plexiglass windows vibrated, pelted by the gale-force rain and spray. All that could be seen through the glass were patches of blurry darkness and spumes of white water, momentarily illuminated by the lights on deck.

Harp staggered to the steering pedestal. He fiddled with the starting buttons for the twin diesels. After a few minutes I was able to detect the vibration of the engines, added to the general cacophony.

"Okay," he announced, "we got power."

I made for the communication gear. No one tried to prevent me from tuning in the weather service. There was a lot of static. I turned up the gain. The recorded voice of the NOAH announcer filled the bridge. It was amazing how much information they managed to pack in a two-minute broadcast.

According to the NOAH forecast Tropical Storm Celeste had finally stopped lolling around in the Gulf and, much to everyone's surprise, had reached hurricane strength at about dawn. That reddest of red dawns. This was a storm that wanted to surprise. It had abruptly shifted direction in midmorning and was now being tracked on a course that would bring the eye of the storm directly over the Lower Keys. The north coast of Cuba was already being severely lashed by high seas, although information was sketchy about the extent of damage. Surveillance aircraft had tracked winds in excess of 120 knots.

I heard Billy mutter, "Holy shit," which about summed it up.

Harp roared with laughter, as if competing with the raw power of the wind.

O'Shea was clinging to a handhold for dear life. I could see the whites of his eyes. He was too frightened to be sick.

"Oh, this is beautiful," Harp crowed. "This is perfect! You got Terrible Teddy and I've got Hurricane Celeste! I'd say we were about even, huh, Murray?"

There were small-craft warnings, big-craft warnings, any-kind-of-craft warnings. The message was clear. Get out of the water and, if at all possible, get your boat out of the water. Evacuation warnings were now being issued for all islands south of Big Pine.

"You picked a great time to come out for a visit," Harp cackled. "We got seventy knots showing already. So that's only what, fifty more to go? I love it! Now watch out you don't OD on that Dramamine, Murray."

Paul from Minnesota had bumped his head coming up the ladder, opening a gash above his eyes. Kate somehow managed to find the first-aid kit and was applying a compress. The boy sobbed quietly, no doubt bitterly regretting the whim that taken him so far from home.

"Harp, stop acting crazy," Kate said, her fingers bloody. "Get on the radio and call the Coast Guard. Let them know we're out here."

He was too busy ragging O'Shea to pay attention. I worked myself along to the shortwave set and pushed the power switch. I expected the little light to come on. It didn't. I tapped the power supply. Still nothing. I pulled out the chassis. The back of the grid was missing. The circuit boards looked like pieces of broken peanut brittle.

I looked at Boone.

"Can it be fixed?" I asked.

He shook his head.

"The citizen band, too?"

He nodded glumly.

Ducat lurched violently, a small craft in increasingly larger seas.

"It was him," he said, pointing a finger at O'Shea. "He told me to."

I got the distinct impression Boone regretted trashing the radio gear and would not now do so, had he to do it over again.

Harp, of course, thought it was a great joke.

18

THE PLAN was that Harp would put the engines in gear and creep forward, winching in the anchor chain as we went. This sounded simple, and would have been, under normal circumstances. Circumstances were anything but normal. Circumstances were winds of seventy knots and increasing, seas maybe fifteen to twenty feet. It was hard to tell, what with the extreme darkness and the driving rain.

The winch fouled almost immediately.

"Not tracking straight," Harp observed. "We'll have to cut the chain."

"Bad idea," I said. "The anchor is the only way to hold the bow into the wind if we lose steerage."

Having opened my big mouth, there was no other option. I volunteered to go down and unfoul the winch and wind the anchor in from the chain locker. No one objected.

Mindy followed me down the ladder. "Want some company?"

"You're going to get wet."

"I'm already wet," she said. "Celeste, I think that's a dumb name for a hurricane, don't you?"

Belowdecks the diesels made almost as much noise as the seas battering the aluminum hull. There was an access to the chain locker on the forward end of the main suite, where Harp and Kate had set up housekeeping. I had to tear apart their bed to get at the hatch. Mindy helped. The boat yawed, spilling us together on the mattress.

"Do we have time for a quickie?" she said.

"You're pulling my leg."

"That's your *leg*? Oh, so it is."

I pulled open the hatch. A foot of water gushed out of the chain locker, soaking the bed. Mindy thought this was very funny. She made a joke about wet blankets. Then she lost her sense of humor when a wave squirted through the hawser holes, catching her full in the face.

"Enough," she sputtered. "Turn off the special effects."

The tiny, V-shaped compartment was wet and wild. I braced myself against the base of the winch. Mindy did likewise. The bow surged up and down in a yawing, unpredictable motion. At the bottom of the arc, water gushed in around the anchor chain, flooding the locker knee-deep.

"Whatever you do, keep your fingers out of the links."

Mindy nodded. I used a pry bar to unfoul the chain. Rewinding was a long, painstaking process. I would wait until the downward plunge created slack, then jam the hydraulic lever down. The winch would begin to turn while Mindy pushed the chain into the track with the pry bar. It took coordination and nerve. Mindy had plenty of both.

"So," I said, spitting out a mouthful of saltwater. "Tell me about Terrible Ted."

She grunted, working the chain into place. "All I know," she said, "is he got off on a murder rap. There was a mug shot of him in O'Shea's file, I assume he's a client of Murray's. I wouldn't have remembered except one time I was in court and my boss pointed out this spooky guy with the slick clothes and he goes, 'Watch out for Terrible Ted, he's a bad actor.' "

The bow plunged down like a thrill ride gone beserk. By then I was so used to being wet I hardly noticed the water gushing through the hawser holes as we fought every yard of that damnable anchor chain.

"Know anything about the other one?" I asked. "Boone?"

Mindy shook her bedraggled head, too out of breath to reply.

"I don't get it," I said. "The salvage operation is being used to launder Del Ray's money, that part makes sense. But how do a couple of thugs like Teddy and Boone figure into what is basically a white-collar crime?"

Mindy said, "Funny thing, I was hoping you could tell me."

"*Moi?*"

"Ought to be easy, for a guy who covers the waterfront."

I decided to shut my mouth while I still had the chance. When it finally swung free, the half-ton anchor struck the side of the hull, rattling us like seeds in a gourd. I crawled out of the chain locker feeling like I'd gone fifteen rounds with Mike Tyson. Numb, exhausted, and outclassed. The mattress was tempting, wet as it was. No time for naps, though, not with the *Ducat* steaming dead into the wind and a pair of hired triggermen waiting on the bridge.

"Any chance the SEC issues firearms to their undercover agents?" I said as we headed for the ladders.

Mindy shook her head.

"No harm in asking," I said.

There was a wrestling match going on when we

got there. Man against machine. Harp was fighting the helm and, from the look of things, slowly losing. He had the diesels at full power, which was the right idea, but the rudder kept lifting out of the water as *Ducat* hobbyhorsed over the crests of the towering seas. Each time a wave pounded into the bow the hull veered a little more off the wind, a little more into the troughs between seas.

"What worries me," Harp said, "she'll want to broach."

O'Shea, sick to the point he could barely move, roused himself to ask what a broach was.

"You don't want to know," I said.

"Means she'll go ass over teakettle," Billy said. "This tub is top-heavy."

O'Shea groaned and doubled over. His bare skull was visible through his thinning red hair. Oddly enough, it was his hard little ears that made him look so weak and vulnerable. "I'm going to die," he announced.

"No way," Harp said. "You're too damn mean."

I worked myself around to the navigator's station. Teddy was strapped into the seat there. Very prudent, was Teddy. Safety first.

I said, "Mind if I sit on your lap, sugar?"

"What do you want?"

No inflection, but I assumed it was a question.

"What I want is to look at the chart and see if there's a way out of here that doesn't involve hitting a reef."

He nodded and undid the seat strap. He timed the roll of the boat, snagging a handhold as he backed away. Neat and clean. No bumps, no bruises. I fastened the strap and unrolled the chart. I was almost surprised to find the Sat-Nav system still functioning. Not that I liked what it had to say.

"We've lost more than a mile," I told Harp. It was

necessary to shout to be heard over the howl of the storm.

"I can't hold her," he shouted back. "I've got the engines at full throttle and it's like we don't have any power."

In a more seaworthy vessel the best bet would have been to claw our way out to open sea and try to ride it out. But *Ducat*, with her flashy superstructure and shallow bottom, had been built to look impressive at the dock, sacrificing her sea-keeping abilities. As Billy had said, she was top-heavy. Turning her ninety degrees to get wind on her quarter would be dangerous, but I saw no other option. We had to make a run for the channel or risk being driven onto the reef.

"You can't do it all at once," I advised Harp. "Ease her five or ten degrees, whatever you can get."

"I'm trying. This wind is crazy."

Indeed it was. The anemometer had maxed out at eighty knots and was no longer functioning. Probably the vanes had been blown right off the stack. I tried to tune in the NOAH broadcast and got only static. Either the *Ducat*'s antenna was down or theirs was. It didn't much matter. You didn't need a weatherman to tell which way Celeste was blowing. The hobbyhorse motion of the hull changed as Harp steered *Ducat* onto the new course. Now it was longer on the way up and longer on the way down. Not much of an improvement. The inclinometer tick-tocked like a lunatic pendulum, registering the sideways tilt of the hull as it careened through the seas. I got tired of watching it and screwed the indicator down tight.

"I'm almost on it," Harp announced. "How far till we clear the reef?"

"Three miles," I said.

The main shipping channel, the cut I had in mind, was the widest opening in the reef. And we would need all the maneuvering room we could find, with the sloppy way *Ducat* was steering.

Billy said, "You're doin' good, bubba. Hang on."

Harp was doing better than good. He was working miracles. Steering a course in dirty weather is never easy, and *Ducat*, overbuilt and underpowered, was a handful. Understeer, and she might take a killing sea over the bows; oversteer, and the hull could veer sideways and broach, capsizing. Harp held the precise and necessary middle ground, anticipating shifts, calculating the effect of wind and wave, his big forearms flexing as he spun the wheel and adjusted the throttle.

Billy said, "We get into the channel, we ought to stick Boone out on the bow, let him shoot off a few flares."

"Shut up," O'Shea said, moaning.

"Hey, you got a point, Murray. We'll stick *you* out there."

It sounded like Billy was contemplating changing sides again. I couldn't blame him. O'Shea and his little entourage had looked like the best bet until Mother Nature played her practical joke. Now power had shifted back to Harper King. O'Shea's boys had guns, but Harp had the helm, and he had the heart.

"Come on, honey," he crooned, working the wheel, finding the point of balance. "Come on, steady now, *steady*."

He almost made it. According to the Sat-Nav, the wind and the pounding seas were driving *Ducat* sideways at a rate of a quarter-mile for every mile she clawed her way parallel to the reef. At that rate we would have had five or six hundred yards to spare as we rounded the mark into the relative safety of the shipping channel.

Would-haves and should-haves. What killed *Ducat* was the Cigarette racing craft O'Shea and his boys had arrived on. Lashed to the side of the hull and forgotten, the Cigarette pounded itself to fragments; in the process it opened a gash in *Ducat*'s thin aluminum skin, just below the waterline.

The first we knew of it was when the starboard diesel began to lose power. Harp reacted by trying to goose the throttle. The engine died.

"I've got lights blinking all over this console," he shouted. "I think we're taking on water."

Ducat was already limping. With the unbalanced port engine at full throttle, steering was even more difficult. I dropped down the ladder to the main deck and found water gushing through the companionway, source unknown. Determined to find and stop what from there looked like a controllable leak, I clambered down a few rungs to the next deck and found myself hip-deep in water. The gash in the side was ten feet long and widening under pressure. The Cigarette boat had been reduced to fiberglass splinters, but the damage was done and could not be rectified. *Ducat* began to list to starboard as the engine room filled.

I went back up with the bad news.

"How much time do we have?" Harp wanted to know. He was milking the port throttle, trying to will life into the remaining engine.

"Not long."

The interior lights flickered. Boone, who had been bearing his seasickness and fear with quiet dignity, suddenly bellowed like a wounded calf. He shut up suddenly, dark Indian eyes fully dilated, when he noticed Teddy stroking the butt of his gun. Giving him warning.

"What about the rafts?" Harp asked me. "Any chance there?"

He meant the containerized survival rafts. There were two four-man rafts on the rear deck, if the waves hadn't torn them loose. I didn't think it was possible to inflate and launch them in waves so steep and violent, and said so.

"Forget the rafts," Billy said, agreeing with me. "Look at this wind! Raft'll be airborne before you can get it over the side."

Harp cursed. I noticed the difference under my feet, the lack of vibration. The port engine was gone. Moments later the lights went out. The wind answered, shrieking higher. Without power, *Ducat* lost steerage and direction. The bow began to turn.

The lights came on again, dimly. Battery power. Even so, it was a signal of hope. *Ducat* was down but not quite out.

"What's the depth here?"

"The sounder is kaput," I said. "On the chart it shows thirty feet under us. Probably more, with the wind surge."

"Maybe she'll carry over the reef. There's a shallow area on the inside, right?"

I held a Bic lighter over the chart. I knew what Harp was getting at. Ever the optimist, he was hoping that the high waters would carry the hull over the reef and deposit us in a shallow-enough area where *Ducat*, swamped, would still have a portion of the superstructure abovewater.

"Shows an average depth of six to eight feet," I said. "Beyond that, it drops off again to thirty."

"What's the bottom like in that shallow area?"

"Gravel."

"Murray," Harp said, "since you're already on your knees, you might try a prayer. The request, Murr old buddy, is we kiss the reef and go aground without too much fuss."

It was a lot to ask. Too much. I looked at my

watch, trying to estimate how much time we had. Calculating how fast *Ducat* was taking on water, divided by distance to the reef, multiplied by wind and wave, not forgetting the exponential factor of luck.

Harp said, "I'll be damned."

Ducat, in her confusion, was turning slowly all the way around, putting her bow into the wind as she was driven backward.

"She's leveling," Harp shouted. "Come on honey," he urged the boat, "give us a kiss and head for the sandy bottom."

It was true. As the hull settled, taking on water, the boat did level a little. I started to believe we might by some miracle actually clear the reef. I seized on it the way a condemned man being strapped into the electric chair seizes on the idea of a permanent power failure. Then a new sound entered into the shrill howl of the storm. An enormous sighing, like deafening static.

Harp shouted, "A kiss! Just a little kiss!"

I was curious. I had to know where the sighing came from. I unlocked the rear hatch. Instantly the door was torn from my hands. I leaned out into the slipstream. At first all I could make out was a kind of vague blackness, punctuated by horizontal torrents of rain driven by the hurricane wind. Gradually, as my eyes adjusted, the enormous sighing sound became visible.

It's funny how the mind works under stress. The first thing I thought of was the cloud of mist that rises under Niagara Falls. A world of sighing fog, as white and unreal as snow in August. Maybe that's why I was smiling when *Ducat* struck the reef stern first.

19 _____

THE HULL screamed. And as *Ducat* lurched backward, tearing her bottom open on the jagged coral, Boone howled in the darkness.

Hoooo-hooooo-hooooo.

I didn't blame him, not a bit. Fear gives certain men a voice; others it renders mute. At elevated levels of fear, courage is as abstract as quantum mechanics, and nearly as incomprehensible. I pulled Mindy into my arms and waited, unable to speak. Waiting to be torn from the boat and dashed into the wind-maddened seas.

Ducat lurched again. We were thrown sideways, ending up under the navigator's table. I didn't try to move. It was as good a place as any. The aluminum plating made the most god-awful sound as the hull grated against the reef. A choir of psychotic angels, drawing fingernails across a sea of slate. Against that, Boone's plaintive, hound-dog cry was almost a comfort.

Mindy clung tight, face buried against my chest. At every lurch of the boat her grip tightened. It is hard to know exactly how much of the experience you retain in a life-threatening situation, how much your mind invents later to sooth the trauma of re-membering. I'm reasonably certain I exhausted all my adrenaline in the first few minutes, that as time passed a calmness came over me. Holding Mindy helped. After a while my breathing synchronized with hers and the trembles subsided.

At some point I was aware that the scream of the hull had lessened into an intermittent grinding noise as the bow lifted and fell. Boone was silent. In the shadowed dimness I could just barely make him out. His arms were wrapped around the helm pedestal, and his mouth was wide open, like a figure in one of Edvard Munch's nightmare paintings.

I thought, He's screamed himself hoarse.

The next thing I noticed was that by some miracle the deck was only slightly canted. Almost steady under us.

Ducat had wedged herself tight into the reef, facing dead into the wind. She was taking the waves head-on, splitting the seas with her bow. The force of the collision had smashed through the upper layers of coral, forming a natural cradle for what remained of the hull. Each succeeding set of waves was driving her higher, lifting the superstructure well above waterlevel. Achieving stability, almost.

Harp crawled to us on all fours. He caught his breath and said, "Some fucking kiss, huh?"

He sounded almost gleeful. Well, why not? We were alive, for the moment. I looked around, counting heads. Kate was comforting Paul, or maybe he was comforting her. Probably a little of each. Boone still clung motionless to the pedestal. O'Shea, Teddy, and Billy Briggs were missing. That was troublesome. Had they been snatched by an errant wave? Were they hiding below? I had no idea. In truth, I was glad to be rid of them, whatever had happened.

Harp squinted at Boone and said, "Remember Joe E. Brown, the guy in the movies used to wail like a siren? He had a mouth like that."

I remembered. And I was disturbed by the utter stillness of Boone. I peeled myself away from Mindy and crawled to him. It was amazing, how still he was. Then I noticed the odd way he was winking at me, and why.

I said, "He's dead."

"Poor guy," Harp said. "His heart must have give out."

"He's been shot," I said. "Right in the eye. No pulse, but he's still bleeding a little."

Just enough to look, in the shadows, like he was winking. I didn't mention the section of skull the bullet had torn loose from the back of his head. I barely glanced at it, for that matter. It is profoundly disturbing to see how insubstantial brains are when loosed from the cranium. Mere jelly.

I checked under Boone's guayabera, looking for his gun. No such luck.

"I think what happened," I said, "the screaming got on Teddy's nerves."

"The bastard," Harp said. "I wonder what he's done with Murray?"

As we soon enough discovered, O'Shea was very much alive, and Billy Briggs, too. It was Harp who correctly surmised their probable whereabouts.

"The gold," he said. "They've gone to check on the gold."

Celeste had stripped me of any feeling for the treasure. Gold was a heavy thing. It would not float. It had no use, here on the reef, in the world of exploding mist, in the place of breaking waves.

I said, "Flare guns. Where are the flare guns?"

Harp didn't care about shooting flares. He was worried about the gold. "The bastards," he said. "They've got something planned."

I said, "Talk sense. That's five hundred pounds of loose coin. What are they going to do, load their pockets and backstroke into Key West? Come on, Harp. Let's try some flares before this tub distintegrates under us."

"You don't know Murray," he said. "He's got something up his sleeve."

There was no reasoning with him. He had the fever. He'd never lost it. That was why he'd been steering like a man possessed. It wasn't to save himself, or Kate, or the rest of the crew. It was to save the gold. Five fish boxes of yellow coins.

I found the flare gun in a drawer under the navigator's table. I loaded up one of the six shells and went out to the observation platform at the rear of the bridge. I avoided looking down, where black seas surged over the reef. The superstructure offered a slight protection from the wind, although the driving rain found a way to sting like a shower of nettles. Not that I'd ever been showered with nettles. If it ever happens, I'll be able to say it feels like hurricane rain.

That's the crazy way I was thinking, out there in the empty howling.

I raised the flare gun and fired. In all I launched four of the six shells. It was a useless gesture, a waste of flares. I staggered back inside, ears ringing from the deafening roar of the wind and found myself shouting, "Well, we know they're not hurricane-proof! We know *that* much!"

None of the flares had gotten more than twenty feet above the top of the superstructure before Celeste slammed them down into the maelstrom. *Poof*! Nary a fizzle. I had barely seen them ignite. Had there been a rescue vessel in the immediate vicinity—highly unlikely—there was no chance of us being sighted.

Mindy took the flare gun from my numb hands. "You're freezing," she said, "and your hand is bleeding again."

So it was. The stiches had opened and a little blood seeped from the wound. Not much. Less than had winked from the hole in Boone's eye. His body remained clinging to the pedestal, jaw hanging open. I took the blanket Mindy had handed me and covered him with it.

Poor, murderous, howling bugger.

"If we're still here when the eye of the storm comes through, we can try the flares again."

Mindy nodded, willing to humor me. She had other plans for the flare gun and tucked it into the waist of her jeans. "In case we want to give Teddy a signal," she explained.

The flare launcher was a kind of weapon. Rudimentary, but better than nothing. I should have thought of that myself before wasting four of the flares. The should-haves were really starting to pile up. Pretty soon I would need a filing system to keep track of them.

"I'm going down there," Harp announced.

"Don't be a fool. Look what happened to Boone. And he was on their side."

"You can do what you like," he said. "I'm going down."

A few more should-haves were added to the pile. We should have stayed on the bridge with Paul, who absolutely refused to move. We should have tied Harp up, if necessary. We should have . . . You get the idea.

Ducat was flooded up to her waterline. The gash on the side was insignificant now; there were gaping holes in her bottom and part of the keel was torn away. The hull resonated with the thrill of the great wind. The bow was more or less intact, and that was taking the brunt of the punishment, absorbing the steady shock of striking waves. That much I could ascertain from the companionway, where the water level had subsided to ankle-deep. It was fairly warm as we sloshed through it. The air inside the boat was humid and thick with the stench of the drowned diesels.

Mindy and I had flashlights and used the beams to feebly penetrate the gloom. Harp hefted a length of pipe he'd wrenched loose from a stanchion. Kate was empty-handed. She was worried about leaving Paul on the bridge.

"Believe me, he's safer up there," I said. "If the hull rolls, he might get to the rafts. Not that a raft is going to do him a lot of good," I added lamely.

"The hull isn't going to roll," Harp insisted. "Solid as a rock."

To demonstrate he splashed his foot against the deck. *Ducat*, in her humor, shifted at exactly that moment. Not a lot, just enough to show us that nothing was rock-solid, not even the reef.

"Proves my point," he said. "We ain't going nowhere."

The pipe made a *pit-pat* sound as he tapped it into the palm of his hand. Like he was warming up to swing for the cheap seats, hit one out of there.

"I don't care about the money," he said. "I really don't."

Not that anyone had asked.

"It's the principle of the thing."

Well, that was comforting. That was how the Civil War began, and why the guns of August were readied—for the principle of the thing. One of these days, when some charismatic geezer gets impatient and launches the final batch of party balloons, we can all die satisfied, knowing it was for the principle of the thing.

And so, against my better judgment, I slogged through the passageway, following Harper King, ex-con and swindler, because I wanted his approval. I didn't think of it that way at the time, of course. I was responding to instinct, to the old tribal loyalties that well up when reason has been abraded by misadventure. Because Harper King was indisputably a leader, a chieftain type. Not for his brawn, strong as he was, and surely not for his brains. The chieftain quality is not easily defined; it may have to do with heart, or passionate intensity, or dream fulfillment. Whatever, the leader attraction is powerful, almost irresistible when you get as near to the mortal edge as we were, traipsing through a dark, ruined hull at the height of a hurricane.

"Murray'll listen to reason," Harp muttered. "He's a lawyer, he has to listen."

Mindy, swinging her flashlight, muttered, "I swear, it sounds like this boat is talking, you know?"

The continuous shock of the pounding waves set up vibrations within the hull. Pinging sounds, metallic creaks, low, groaning complaints; an almost human voice emerged from the fabric of the ruined yacht. As we approached the access to the rear deck, the voices became quite real.

"The fuck I will."

That was Billy Briggs, and he didn't sound happy.

"Y'all keep that trigger-happy bastard away from me, heah?"

No, not happy at all. I motioned to Mindy to kill her flashlight. We hugged the wall and followed along. Harp whistled tunelessly under his breath. I didn't have the heart to shut him up. What was the point? If you're backing into the dragon's den with your rump exposed, you might as well whistle a few bars before the beast exhales and turns you into a charcoal briquet.

We turned the corner. The hatchway to the rear deck was open. Sheets of rain and spray poured down. In the relative protection of the companionway a lantern threw shadows along the wall. One of the shadows was Billy. He had a fish box full of gold in his arms. Murray O'Shea was holding the lantern.

Teddy, no surprise, had the gun.

Billy said, "I ain't playing nigger for nobody. Might's well get that straight right now. Old Terrible here wants to shoot me, let him go ahead and do it. Then y'all can drown in each other's arms, 'cause you sure as hell ain't gettin' off this wreck without me."

"Billy," O'Shea said, "calm yourself."

"I'll calm myself when your boy points his pea-shooter somewheres else."

O'Shea caught sight of Harp and swung the lantern at us. Behind him Billy swore and lowered the fish box to the deck.

Harp waded forward, splashing the water underfoot like he was having the time of his life, and said, "He's always bitching about something, ain't he, Murray? Tell you what, Bill, I'll give you a hand with those boxes if that'll make you feel better."

"Well, well," O'Shea said. "Isn't this a surprise."

"You must be feeling better," Harp said. "Got over your seasickness, I mean."

"More or less," O'Shea said. "It helps to keep busy."

Harp laughed. "Keeping busy, I love it. What I come down here for, what I want to remind you, I'm still captain of this vessel."

It was O'Shea's turn to laugh. A flat *hee hee hee*, lacking even a trace of levity.

"And what does being 'captain' mean," he said, "exactly?"

"It means I don't like it when someone on my vessel gets an extra hole put in his head, like Boone did. It means, Murray, old buddy, old pal, I'd like to know what the fuck you're doing, trying to rip me off."

A sea broke over the rear deck and surged up into the companionway. O'Shea, being the shortest, got soaked the worst. He didn't like it. It put the fear of the storm back in him and wound his mainspring a few clicks tighter.

"Okay," he said, his voice rising an octave. "We're going to quit fucking around here. Billy, escort these people to some other part of this leaky goddamn boat. I don't care where, I just want them out of my sight."

Harp ignored him. He had his own slant on reality and he wasn't quite ready to make the necessary adjustment. "You're way out of line, Murray, ordering him around like that. Billy works for me, right, Bill?"

"Yeah, right. Now gimme that." With his left hand, Billy snatched the flashlight from Mindy's hand before she could react. In his right was the snub-nosed .38 with the cheap nickel plating. "Y'all turn around now and march back the way you come."

"Hey, Billy?"

"Drop that piece of pipe, Harp. I ain't foolin' now. Terrible Ted ain't the only one can pull a trigger around here."

"You'd shoot me, Bill?"

Billy said, "Sure. Now y'all drop that pipe like I axed. Good. Now march. Hup, two, like in the marines."

He kept ten feet or so behind us. Enough so I didn't quite dare to turn and leap for his gun hand. Not that I thought Billy had it in him to be an executioner, not in cold blood. That was more Teddy's style. But Bill was more than capable of locking us up inside the battered hull, and that would amount to the same thing, eventually. Given time, the pounding waves would find a way to crack open *Ducat* and scatter her pieces into the waters beyond the reef.

Kate said, "Bill, it's not too late to change your mind."

"Hush up," he said.

"Murray is using you," she said. "He uses everyone."

"I say hush up, I mean it."

We were in the bow section of the boat, not far from the main suite, when Mindy stumbled. As she regained her balance, she came up with the flare gun and popped one at Billy Briggs. The flare hit him square in the chest and bounced off, sizzling as it hit the ankle-deep water.

By then I was launched. I collided with his arm, letting my momentum carry me through and down. The revolver and the flashlight both skittered away. Billy landed on his back in the water, with my legs sprawled over his. With the flashlight out, the darkness closed like a fist.

Right away I knew it wasn't going to be a repeat of the silly fistfight outside the Pirates Den. Billy Briggs sober was not a staggering, mindless fool. In the darkness he did not resort to the wild, roundhouse swings he'd thrown outside the topless bar. He went right for the throat. His thumb pressed against my larynx and made me see sparkles in the dark.

Pretty sparkles. I was in the bottom of a deep well and voices echoed down, falling like flecks of light. "Do something quick," the voices urged me. I snapped my teeth shut and felt something soft crunch between them. Billy screamed and let go of my throat. I rolled away, splashing into the layer of water and the soggy carpet.

"Find the gun."

That's what I tried to say. It came out as a croaking noise. Before I could make myself clear, he was on me again, fists pounding into my abdomen. I reacted, pulling my knees up. He grunted and the wind rushed out of him.

Score one for my side.

He wanted my throat again. His probing hand found my jaw. I bit down hard and tasted blood. Billy screamed. I brought my right hand up sharply and caught him somewhere near his solar plexus, choking the scream off. Then I tried to find his eyes with my thumbs.

A boxing match it wasn't. This was a dirty-down, no-holds-barred, roll-in-the-dark battle for life. I missed his eyes just as he got a handful of my hair and slammed the back of my head against the deck.

More pretty, tingling stars. I yanked both fists up and caught what felt like a cheekbone. The hand unwove itself from my hair. I tried the same place again and missed.

The lights came back on. Mindy had located one of the flashlights. Billy saw me and launched himself like a maddened swamp gator. I kicked, splashing him in the eyes. He shot by, hooking the crook of his arm under my chin.

I wrenched free, managed to get up on my knees, and swung with all my might. Billy ducked. My knuckles squibbed over his crew cut. His fist jabbed out and caught me just above the heart. I was falling back as he struck, or that might have done it, right there.

Mindy got into the act and brought the flashlight down hard on the top of Billy's head. I don't know exactly what happened next because the light went out again. There was a wild, boarlike grunting. When Mindy got the flashlight back on, I saw that Harp had Billy by the seat of the pants and was trying to heft him up and bash his head into the wall.

Attaboy, Harp. Flatten that crew cut.

Billy was no lightweight, however, and his shifting mass and the slick carpet threw Harp off. His feet went out from under. Billy dropped, and it was Harp's head that connected with the wall. The big guy sighed and his eyes rolled up. He was out of it for the moment, seeing stars all his own.

"Mindy, find the gun!"

Like she wasn't already trying. She crouched, flashlight clamped between her teeth, running both hands over the deck. Coming up empty.

Meantime, Billy tried to kick a field goal with my head. I did my best turtle imitation and the foot whistled by, nicking my ear. Now it was Billy's turn to lose his balance. He upended, landing hard on his ass. Kate had crept up behind him and let him have it, straight down on the top of his head with her fists locked together.

Ouch! I thought, but Billy shook it off, shoving her roughly back. She skidded down the carpet, floundering, choking on a mouthful of water.

"Bitch!" he screamed, turning to follow her down.

I grabbed his shoulder and spun him to face me. Cat-quick, he let go a punch that caught me in the gut just as my fist flattened his nose.

A broken nose produces a impressive quantity of blood. Some react by fainting dead away, others become more enraged. Billy fit in the latter category. He roared and threw himself at me, trying to land blows with both fists at once.

I ducked under him and connected with a solid head butt. Now his tongue was cut and his eyes got that hot, glowy look. The last barrier was down. He wanted only one thing, and that was to kill me.

"Don't!" I shouted.

That was for Kate, who had regained her feet and was coming at him from behind. Billy saw her and swung his fist backward, connecting solidly to her jaw.

Kate folded. And Billy charged me, coming low like a linebacker, launched from the balls of his feet. A hundred and eight-five pounds of rage. I dropped under him, bucking my knees up, and heard his head slam into the bulkhead.

A normal human being would have had the sense to pass out. Not Bill. Groggy, unable to get to his feet, he came at me on all fours, teeth barred, blood dripping from his chin. Swamp Thing himself.

Weapon of choice would have been an elephant gun. Lacking that, I backed up and got ready to try kicking him in the throat.

The next thing I knew the deck was flipping out from under my feet. I thought Mindy was screaming, but it was the hull, tearing sideways against the reef, careening at a steep angle. The flashlight went out for the last time and I was airborne in the darkness.

20

I WAS drowning at the bottom of the sea. I was blind, yet somehow aware of the hammerhead coming at me from behind, teeth glowing like golden spikes in the black sea night. All around us a thousand small fish made a thousand small, screeching noises.

The thing about regaining consciousness in the dark is, you can't be sure you're not just dreaming of being awake. I didn't need to pinch myself because I hurt all over. The screeching noise was *Ducat* being driven sideways along the reef. The drowning part was the water washing over me as the hull tipped at a steep angle. The shark, well, the shark is always there, waiting on the other side of sleep.

There was an egg-sized lump on my temple, but not much blood, from the feel of it. My body felt like it had been run through the rinse cycle in a washing machine owned by Norman Bates. Never mind, no limbs had been fractured and I still had all eight fingers and both thumbs. I assumed my eyes were still functional, although it was hard to tell in the inky dark.

Screeeeeeeeeee

Ducat inched sideways. She'd gone on her beam ends, canted at about forty-five degrees. I was able to distinguish wall from deck because the deck was covered with soggy carpet. As to which way I was facing, that was anybody's guess. No, it wasn't, it was mine alone. Pick a direction, Mr. Egghead. Get moving. Because if this hull decides to slide off the reef the only direction is death everlasting, amen.

I called Mindy's name. No response. It was unlikely she'd be able to hear me above the deafening noise of aluminum scratching itself to death on the coral. I gave up shouting and slogged along through cool, knee-deep water. One foot on the deck, the other braced against the wall. Thank K-Mart for cheap sneakers; wet, they had more traction than the designer boat shoes that are de rigueur at the yacht club.

I moved in a sort of crouch, arm extended into the blackness, trying to picture the layout of the boat. If I was heading toward the stern, as hoped, the passageway would make an abrupt turn to my right. I got the hang of the scuttling ape walk that was necessary to keep balance, and picked up the pace, expecting—hoping—to bump into a bulkhead.

What I bumped into was a warm body. Before I could react, two powerful arms swept around me and began to apply bone-crushing pressure. After a few thundering heartbeats I realized the headlock was meant to be a hug.

"Who've I got?"

It was Harper King, sounding as spooked as I felt.

"I give up," I said. "Whatever game this is, you win."

"Stash! I thought maybe it was Billy. He was ahead of me when we started to run."

"You hear anyone else?"

"Can't hear nothing but that scrapin' noise, and the storm. Hang on, I wanna look atcha."

There was a spark and a small glow. Harp's cleft chin appeared in the flicker of a disposable lighter. He grinned and I suddenly felt a whole lot better.

"Helluva mess I got us in, hey, bubba?"

"It's been . . . different," I said. "How far you been along here?"

"Back a ways. It drops off toward the companion-way."

I said, "Let's go."

Harp shook his head. "She's flooded. Can't get through that way, not without scuba gear."

It made sense, in the crazy way of things. We were on the high side of the hull now. The exit to the rear deck was amidships, presumably underwater.

"What about Mindy and Kate?" I asked.

"They were ahead of me, with Billy right behind 'em. Screamin' bloody murder. Good thing, too. I think he chased 'em out before we got turned this far."

I said, "You think?"

"Hell, no. I'm positive. They made it out."

I wanted to believe him, and did. The alternative was not a matter that bore consideration.

We agreed to head for the bow, in hopes that access to the deck through the master suite was still viable. That way proved futile when we found the first watertight hatch jammed shut. Harp bruised his big shoulders trying, but there was really no hope of cracking it open. The way the hull had twisted, it would take a cutting torch to get through.

"Better quit flicking that Bic," I advised. "We may need it later."

Harp thought that was pretty funny. "What are you expecting, a box of Havana cigars is going to float by, we can light up?"

"The hull shifted over this far. Maybe it'll shift back, the right combination of seas hits her."

He liked the theory. Give Harper King a grain of hope and he'd work it up to nugget size. His partic-ular loupe on life made a chip of rhinestone look like a diamond as big as the Ritz. But when we worked ourselves back toward the stern, we found the flood-waters at about the same level, if not a little higher.

No problem; Harp had a new and improved theory.

"The eye of this storm is going to pass over us any minute now. When it comes, the seas are bound to recede. We'll be high and dry, right?"

There was no guarantee of any such thing happening, but I agreed just to make him happy. And because in the dread-filled dark I wanted the comfort of his undaunted heart.

As it happened, his theory about the approaching eye of the hurricane was right on the money. We were sitting with our back against the tilted wall, conserving our strength and our air, which was starting to feel flatter and less satisfying with every breath. Suddenly his big hand closed over my wrist and squeezed hard enough to hurt.

"Listen," he said. "Ain't that a beautiful sound?"

The beautiful sound was silence. *Ducat* had stopped screeching along the reef, and the wind that had been driving the seas, resonating through the up-turned hull, that wind had suddenly died.

"I just got a feeling," Harp said, "things are going to work out."

He crawled over and inspected the submerged passageway. "Still too much water," he reported. "But she'll go down, given time."

No point mentioning that we didn't have much of that particular resource. Depending on the course of the storm, the eye would pass over in, at most, an hour. If the tidal surge was going to drop, it would have to do so soon, to be of any use to us. Meantime, all we could do was wait, lulled by the intermittent creaking of the broken hull.

Maybe it was the darkness that made Harp want to confide in me, or the spooky quiet, or because I was trustworthy, brave, and true. Whatever the reason, he told me all about his felony conviction and the circumstances that preceded it.

"Right up until that gavel came down, I was sure they'd find me innocent. Or at least suspend the sentence, which is what O'Shea, that fuck, promised would happen. It wasn't like I'd used a gun to rob anyone. You want to take money off an orthodontist, all you gotta do is talk dirty, he'll start throwing checks at you."

Talking dirty, he explained, had nothing to do with sex. It was the idea of risk-taking as excitement.

"These dentists I sold to, you gotta understand, they were begging me to take their moeny. I'd tell 'em, I'd say, 'We're talking ninety-day options, not four-star bonds.' I'd say, 'This is a high risk venture. This option is a three-month roll of the dice, Doc, and at the end you might come up snake eyes.' They loved to hear that kind of talk. Gambling talk, race-track talk. I'd say, 'She's a filly with class coming up on the outside,' okay? And what I'm referring to is an option on a company makes auto parts. It didn't matter. To these guys the idea of risking ten grand was more exciting than all the bare tits on Lauderdale beach. Twenty grand was even better. I'd talk to these guys and I'd hear it in their voices, that excitement. They wouldn't, very few of 'em would dare to drop a C-note on a long shot at Hialeah, okay? But give 'em a chance to blow ten large on an option for a stock they'd never heard of, I'm telling you, Stash, these guys couldn't wait to get to the bank, give me a certified check."

I said, "You really thought O'Shea would get you off?"

"Sure. Why not? I mean, he got Teddy off, right? And Teddy had a couple of priors and also there was three different eyewitnesses saw him gun down this poor stiff got mixed up in some drug deal. It went sour and Teddy got hired to take him out."

"Three eyewitnesses? O'Shea must be one hell of a lawyer, he sets his mind to it."

"Well, I think what happened, Teddy kind of helped himself. He made bail and Murray kept delaying the trial, and when they finally get into court, surprise, none of the witnesses are available for testimony."

"Old Ted scared 'em away, huh?"

"Even better. Teddy made 'em disappear, all three. As in from the face of the earth."

"He killed them?"

"I assume he killed them first. With Teddy you never know. I heard a couple of different versions. One involved a sausage factory, the other a fish-processing plant. I guess Ted, he doesn't like to see anything wasted, he wanted to recyle those witnesses into some kind of food product."

"Jesus."

"Like I say, it was Murray got bail set low enough to spring him, so Teddy could resolve his problem with the eyewitnesses. Then he stands up there, Murray does, tells the judge life is full of coincidences. The special prosecutor is so pissed he's chewing on his briefs—that's a pun, Murray had to explain it to me—but what can they do? They got no witnesses, they got no case. Teddy walks."

"And you got two years."

"Well, it was a different kind of case. The way it came down, with Freddie Del Ray out of the picture, they were looking for people they could lock up for a while. Justify the cost of the investigation. Anybody even slightly associated with Del Ray—and I met him exactly once, everything with him was always through lawyers—anybody smelled faintly of Del Ray, they went after us. They even indicted a couple the people worked on that big estate of his up in Palm Beach, misappropriation of household accounts or something. So when they finally get around to me, they sit me down, and all very polite, they say, 'It's up to you, Mr. King, sir. You can take your chances with a jury trial. Do that, however, and we'll be obliged to indict Miss Starling. Which they knew they had me over a barrel, right there.''

"So you pleaded and took the two."

"What choice did I have?"

He said that without a trace of irony. Like there really hadn't been any choice. In his sand-castle world, carefully constructed to shield himself from cold reality of incoming tides, the Golden Boy did not betray the Golden Girl, even if he himself had been betrayed and manipulated. Harper King, I realized, conned no one so well as he conned himself.

"Know how I met her? Kate?" Harp's voice softened. "She made a cold call on me, can you believe it?"

"Cold call?"

"I had this car-leasing gig, working more or less independent for an Orlando outfit, covers most of the state. Set up a booth at a mall in Pompano. Little slide show of the various vehicles available. Bimmers, mostly, that was the hot car in Pompano. You'd think it would be Caddys, but it was BMWs. So anyhow, you have the pictures of the cars, you have the credit applications, you have the telephone to check with the main office and the bank they run the credit through. The cut you make, on a deal like that, is you get the half the deposit and first month's payment. It's a hustle, but what the hell, it was an honest hustle, you know?"

In a way I did. I'd never sold cars, or leased them, but in a way fish-guiding is an honest hustle. Which is probably why I'm so lazy about it.

"Okay, how I met Kate, this knockout blonde comes into the booth and takes a seat at my little desk there," Harp said. "Right away my day brightened up. You've seen Kate—I mean, the immediate impression is class, brains, looks, and legs. Not necessarily in that order. So I say, what else, 'How can I help you,' just an opening, right? I'm definitely in no rush to close a sale with this lady. The idea, make it last. Right away I figure her for the Mercedes coupe. Six hundred a month on a five-year lease, option to buy, you pick up the balloon."

"The balloon?"

"Balloon payment. Never mind. Point is, Kate wasn't there to lease a car. She's there, get this, to sell me an annuity. Dressed beautiful, you know, and with those incredible eyes, first thing she says, 'How's business? Can you make any money in this lease racket?' Which some people want to be reassured, anybody they do a deal with is successful, it reflects on them, so I say, 'hey, this is a high-end business, I'm moving more paper than the guy at the newstand.' Okay, I say that, I get this incredible smile. I could, I swear, feel my blood pressure go up about twenty points, she turns that smile on me. And she's smiling because Harper King, who knows every sales scam going, has just put his foot in her trap.

"Kate says, 'You're clearing that much, have you given any thought about making informed investments?' And she opens this little Gucci briefcase she's got and lays this brochure on me, this annuity plan she's selling. It was beautiful. What a move! This lady had guts enough to try a cold call on me, you had to love it."

"So," I said, "you sold each other."

"Nah, *she* sold *me*. I signed up for the annuity plan. Even paid the first payment, so Kate would get her commission. By the time the second payment was due we were shacked up together, I let it go. We had big plans by then. Kate heard about this gig selling options for the Del Ray Group, we were setting that up. Which was a great deal, a beautiful deal, except Del Ray, this big financial wizard with the polo ponies and the yachts, he decides to bolt and left me and a lot of other guys holding the bag. Anyhow, you know what happened there. I had to do a deuce. That wasn't any fault of Kate's. She's a great girl, Stash. The best."

I had to agree with him. If I hadn't, he might have torn my head off, or worse, believed me. It seemed like a good idea to veer the conversation away from the love of his life. So I asked if King-Ducat Salvors was one of Del Ray's schemes.

"Nah, this is my baby all the way," he said. "What happened, I first got the idea out of a book. I never read much until I got in there, the facility library. Who am I kidding, the *prison* library. One day I pick up *Treasure Diver's Guide*, by this guy Potter, and what he did was list all the known ships went down with cargo of value. And there are, like *hundreds* of them, okay? Some have been salvaged, most haven't. So I started requesting any book with 'treasure' in the title, and there must be hundreds of those, too. It gets me thinking, just to pass the time, how I'd been scuba diving since I was a kid and all I ever looked for was fish to spear, or lobster. All the time there's even, eight hundred million in gold down there. Waiting for the Cousteau and his pals to invent the Aqualung, right? And it ain't just here off Florida, Stash. We pick this reef clean and there's a whole 'nother world waiting down in the Amazon. I read this book, about how the Incas fled from the mountains and took their gold into the Amazon wilderness. It's just waiting there, wealth untold . . . "

Harp sighed deeply, contemplating his fantasy. "So, anyway, I get kind of fixed on the idea that searching for sunken treasure will be a hell of a lot more fun, and I'm pretty sure less risky, jailwise, than selling bogus options."

Less risky, jailwise. That was a typical Harperism. And the idea of searching for Inca gold in the Amazon, that had to be original. In the dark I grinned to myself.

"So what happens, I sell Murray on the idea. This is while I'm still inside. All we need, I tell him, is a boat and a wreck location, we're in business. When I get out, old Murr has come through. He's got *Ducat* on loan from Freddie Del Ray. Anyhow, that's what I thought. Only now it turns out, Murray, the little shit, finagled the boat loose from some corporation of Freddy's, he's down there on Cayman counting his money, he doesn't even know what we've been doing. As far as he knows, the feds seized *Ducat* when he skipped."

"What?" I said. "I thought Del Ray was the backer. Getting a big cut. I, um, overhead you discussing it with O'Shea one night."

"You did, huh?" Harp chuckled. "Hell, we got loud enough I guess the whole crew heard. Point is, that's what I thought, too, that Freddie had put up the seed money. That's what Murray *wanted* me to think. Like Del Ray gets seventy-five percent off the top for the boat and expenses. Only it's Murray who was getting the seventy-five. That's why he was such a tight ass about expenses. So far he's taken, what, almost six hundred grand out. Which, in comparison to what we scored on the bottom, is peanuts."

I asked, as tactfully as possible, how he had known about the coins. U.S. Mint gold pieces unrelated to the galleon or any other known wreck.

"Are you kidding?" he said. A laugh started deep

in his belly. "You think I planned that? Man, I had no idea! What it was, I'm pretty sure, it was a gift from the gods. Old Neptune is saying, 'Harp you screwed up and you took your punishment, and now we're making it up to you. Only you gotta take the stuff and run, because this dame Celeste is mighty pissed that I give you her jewelry.' Which we would have made it back if it wasn't for Billy getting on the horn to Murray, they decide to engineer a rip-off, leave me holding the bag again."

That brought us to the subject of Billy Briggs. How exactly had he chosen Briggs as his divemaster?

"Kate found him. Murray was Billy's lawyer, see, and Kate got to know him that way. She told me, Kate did, she came for a visit to the facility, the prison, she tells me she's got this project named Billy Briggs. He's got a lot of rough edges, she's going to polish him up a little, he can work for us. Kate was the sales manager, trained the staff when we first got together. She's good at it, the best. Only we didn't need a salesman for the treasure gig, exactly; what we needed was a diver knew the Lower Keys. Which Billy did. Also he knew about this old dude, Ben Jones, had this wreck location he might part with cheap. See, it was essential we have a wreck to dive on. You have a wreck, maybe pull up a few doubloons, you can make a good pitch to investors. You have to show 'em some gold."

It was all starting to make sense. Briggs had been in it from the beginning, when King-Ducat was no more than a jailbird daydream to sustain Harper King. Kate Starling had taken care of everything; she and Bill and Murray O'Shea, setting it up for Harp to apply his patented, optimistic spin on the deal when he got out. The salvage company was a near-perfect cover, according to O'Shea. Way better than Del Ray's boiler-room swindle of selling bogus stock options. They would be selling dreams this time out, and if the dream of finding gold didn't come true, the SEC would have one hell of a job trying to prosecute.

It was a nice little money machine until Harp screwed up the works by recovering gold, actual gold. The proceeds of which would have to be split with the shareholders. And the staties and the feds would be there in line, waiting for their percentage.

"Murray's going to cut and run. Billy told him about the gold, his first reaction is to take it off me, keep the whole cake. I can smell it on his breath. And Terrible Ted is going to clean up the crumbs. Hell, no one else knows what we found. It's a perfect rip."

There was one flaw in Murray O'Shea's plan to hijack the gold. A flaw with winds in excess of a hundred knots and seas powerful enough to batter *Ducat* into scrap aluminum. The getaway boat— another gift from the unknowing Del Ray—had already been destroyed. That left the life rafts and *Ducat*'s motor launch.

"Teddy knows what he's doing," Harp said. "He drove the Cigarette, which means he can read a chart, or at least use the Loran. Nearest key from where we sit is what, eighteen miles?"

"Something like that."

"Low little hull like that, you go with it, don't try to fight the seas, you just might make it."

I said, "You might, assuming you can reach shore before the back end of the storm hits."

Harp ignored me. "Hear that?" he said.

"Hear what?"

"The water lapping. It sounds different, somehow. What I think, bubba, we'd best check her out."

21 _____

HARP LEANED out into the dark corner where the passageway turned, holding the lighter. He looked down and flashed his gold-tinted grin at me.

"Bingo," he said. "Level has dropped seven or eight feet."

I crawled to the edge and looked down the steep incline. For once Harp wasn't exaggerating. The floodwater was lapping just above the exit into the companionway.

"How far is it, you figure?"

I knew what Harp was driving at. How far would we have to free-dive to make it out to the rear deck? I tried to picture the companionway, the cabin doors on either side. Counting the strides it would take to walk through it in my mind.

"Something like twenty-four feet," I said. "Give or take."

Harp slapped me on the back. "Piece of cake," he said. "Swim it in your sleep."

"There may be debris in the way. Wreckage spilled from the starboard cabins."

"Hell, twenty feet," he said, ignoring my warning about debris. "That ain't far enough to be considered a dive, really. I bet you could swim a hundred, you had to."

"I'm not a pearl diver, Harp."

"Just as well. Shortage of oysters down there. Tell

you what, I'll go first, any junk in the way, I'll bust it loose."

He entrusted the Bic to me. Like he was passing a torch. Always the grand gesture, the dramatic pose. I expected a crisp salute when he dropped down the incline and was not disappointed. I leaned out with the lighter and wished him luck. He nodded, treading water, and began to gulp in air, hyperventilating.

I said, "Break a leg," and saw him smile. His feet thudded against the bulkhead as he pushed off. The black water shimmered and he was gone.

Give him time enough to get through . . .

I followed the interminable progress of the luminous second hand as it circumnavigated the face of my watch, and was shocked to discover it was two in the morning. I waited three minutes, then tucked the Bic into my back pocket and dropped down the incline.

The water was colder than I remembered it. That may have been something to do with not having eaten for more than sixteen hours; my body thermostat was getting out of whack. Taking the cue from Harp, I treaded water and gulped air. The point being to enrich the blood with oxygen. Good for an extra yard or two when free-diving.

Lungs full, I dropped under the water, found the bulkhead with my feet, and pushed forward. Almost immediately I bumped into a cabin door that was ajar. It was a fairly simple matter to work my way around it, but the mere fact made my heart hammer that much harder.

Save your panic . . .

That's what a good dive instructor will teach you. Push the little demon into the back of your mind. Slam the lid on him. If he gets loose, Panic will fight and kick until he's found a way to drown you. And it needn't be in deep water. Panic can turn off your lights in a foot or two of water, if you let him throw a tantrum.

I pulled myself along the companionway, lungs burning. Ahead, miles away, was a faint, barely discernible patch of light. Panic had his skeletal fingers under the lid, pushing to break loose. The blood in my ears sang like a hymn.

"Like a dirge," Panic said.

I kicked, feet banging against the sides, fingers clawing the slick carpet, reaching for yards, then feet, then inches. Into faint light.

My head cleared the exit. I swooped my cupped hands, fighting for the surface six feet above. And I did not move. The demon was loose, he was holding me back, dragging me down.

What happened, my shirt collar snagged on the hatch handle. Chalk up another should-have. I kicked and twisted to no avail. My lungs gave up. Exploding with pain. Unendurable pain. I was ready to inhale seawater just to stanch the fire inside, when something big and dark came down at me. Steel fingers grabbed my shoulders, ripping the shirt off my back, yanking me loose. Suddenly I was flying up, breaking the surface.

Breathing air.

Funny thing, for the first couple of minutes it hurt almost as much as not breathing. The difference was it was nice pain, alive pain.

"Looked like you was doing some kind of funny dance down there," Harp said. "The way your arms and legs were moving."

"Thanks," I said. It was the second time Harper King had saved my life.

"Well, he said, "don't be too thankful. You may notice you're out of the frying pan and into the fire."

I blinked the saltwater from my eyes and saw Teddy sitting partway up the outside ladder. Teddy and his guns. He had one in his right hand and another—Boone's, I assumed—tucked in his belt. Over him, incredibly, was a patch of open sky, illuminated by a three-quarter moon.

The night air was impossibly still. The calm inside the hurricane had an eerie, feral quality. The scent was rich and heady, almost dreamlike, but I knew better than to trust it. The sea was merely holding its breath; soon enough it would exhale. When that happened, the other arm of the storm would swing through, blotting out the moon and the stars, turning the world to wind again.

"Mindy?"

"Ted has put her to work. Her and Kate. See, Ted has taken the high ground. He's got us covered and at the very same time he's keeping an eye on the girls. Ain't that right, Ted?"

Ted smiled ever so faintly. I dragged myself out of the water and found a foothold on the steeply slanted deck. The seas, though no longer wind-torn, were still immense. Huge, loping swells, breaking endlessly at the crest. The peaks towered over *Ducat* and I could feel her bow rising and falling as if the swells intended to lift her broken hull and fling it clear of the reef, given time.

Teddy motioned with his revolver. "Up that way," he said, soft enough so I had to strain my waterlogged ears to hear him. "Keep your hands in sight," he added.

Harp followed behind me, whistling the tune to "Camptown Races." "Doo-da, doo-da," he added at the chorus. "Oh, doo-da-day."

Mindy, catching sight of us, let out a small, happy scream. She had a galvanized bucket in her hands, full of something that glinted in the moonlight. "I told you, Kate," she shouted. "I said they'd be okay! Oh, Stash, honey, you're all scratched up."

It was true. Bashing around in the submerged companionway had left superficial damage. Scrapes and scratches and places where bruises would take form. The stitches in my hand had opened again. Didn't matter. I was so damn glad to feel the open air and see the moonstruck sky that I couldn't feel anything but good.

Billy Briggs glowered at me. His nose was sort of mashed and a few new dents showed through his crew cut, but he appeared to be as functionally ferocious as ever. He'd lost that snub-nose .38, though, and it was costing him. Without an equalizer he was relegated to helping the rest of the slaves, passing up buckets of coins, and he didn't look pleased.

"Hey, Murray," Harp shouted, "are we having fun yet?"

The attorney was seated in the motor launch, wearing an orange life jacket. The launch was still attached to the davits, a good distance from the water, but O'Shea had found comfort there. The gold was being passed up in stages, bucket by bucket, and he was securing it in the bilge of the little boat.

He passed an empty bucket back down, then addressed Harp. "The way I figure, this makes us even."

"How's that, Murr?"

"*Ducat* was appraised at a little under four million, and right now I'd say she's worth, roughly, nothing whatsoever. You wrecked her, so you owe me."

"Yeah? I was under the impression this tub belonged to Freddie Del Ray."

"Don't quibble, Harper. Del Ray owes me, that's why I had a lien on *Ducat*. *He* owes me, so now *you* owe me. I'm taking the proceeds of, uhm, your little adventure—like I say, we'll call it even."

Harp laughed. "You're a real sport, Murr. And

I'm impressed, you look kinda cute in that life jacket. Only thing, I don't think it's bullet-proof. So when your pal Teddy decides to tie up the last of the loose ends, you better bend over, put your head between your legs, and kiss your sorry Irish ass good-bye."

I couldn't see O'Shea well enough to read his expression. The bantering tone of voice could have been from excitement, or maybe Harp really was getting to him. If he was worried about controlling Teddy, you couldn't blame him. I'd sooner play with a pinless grenade.

"Ted and I have an understanding," O'Shea said. "He needs me. I got him off that time, I can do it again, if necessary."

Harp kept at him. "Think about it, Murr. They'll be serving you with grits on the side. O'Shea Sausage, specially spiced. Teddy doesn't need a lawyer, not when he's got access to that sausage machine."

Billy decided he'd had enough of being ignored. He hoisted himself out of the hold and pulled himself up level with the motor launch. "Hey, Murray? If you all through shootin' the shit, maybe we could get ready to lower this boat."

Harp interrupted his whistling chorus of "Camptown Races" to say, "They signed you on for this little cruise, huh, Bill? You sure about that?"

Billy ignored him. He reached for the davit controls, then froze when Teddy ordered him to back off. He appealed to O'Shea, "All I want is safe passage, Murray. You two decide to cheat me out of my share, I can't stop you."

"Relax," O'Shea said, eyeing Teddy. "You'll get what's coming to you."

"You need me," Billy said, a tone of pleading in his voice. "You want to get this dinky little boat to shore in one piece, you need me. I know these waters. You don't get to high ground before the back end of that hurricane hits us, you ain't gotta snowball's chance."

It was amazing, the way each of them claimed to be needed by the others. O'Shea needed Teddy to act as strong arm and, quite plainly, executioner. Teddy needed O'Shea to keep him out of jail, or so the lawyer hoped. They both needed Bill Briggs to help pilot the launch, or that was what Billy hoped.

There was a whole lot of need and hope going around, and not much time to work things out. Billy was right about the back end of Celeste. Already there were faint stirrings in the night air and high clouds racing against the moon.

"I said relax," O'Shea said. "Get the last few buckets up here, we'll be on our . . . What the hell!"

The launch swung on the davits, responding to a change in *Ducat*'s rocking motion. A set of remarkably large swells had begun to roll through, lifting *Ducat*'s bow, pushing her backward. Gradually, a few feet each lift, the hull was slipping off the reef.

Teddy came down off his perch. A nimble leap brought him to the motor launch. "Get on up here," he barked, pointing the automatic at Mindy and Kate. "Hand up those last two buckets."

Ducat shifted again, twisting her decks around to a less-severe angle. Harp fell to his knees. Mindy slipped and bumped her elbow. I swung around, clutching the rail, trying to keep an eye on Teddy, hoping he would fall.

No such luck. The man was as surefooted as a mountain goat.

"Over on that side," he said, backing carefully around the launch. "You're going to put those buckets inside, then you're going to listen to my count. On three, you all push, let her clear the rail. Billy, you let the brake off the winch."

"Teddy," O'Shea cried. He was in the swinging launch, hanging on with both hands.

"Stay right there," Teddy told him. "Stay down low."

Ducat was still seeking to level herself as she slipped into deeper water. Wanting to keep her head up as the seas poured into her torn hull and sucked her under.

"Do as I say," Teddy said, "or I start shooting."

He was on the opposite side of the launch. Maybe he didn't see what Kate had in her hand as she came up with the last bucket. Maybe he saw it and didn't know what it was: the bang stick, the shark killer Harp had given me.

"Bill, you let out that brake," Teddy ordered. "Now push her clear."

The launch swung on the davits, banging into the rail. Billy popped the winch brake. The little boat dropped about eight feet before stopping with a jerk that made O'Shea scream like a girl. With attention focused on the swaying launch, Kate sidled closer, keeping the weapon at her side. I crawled toward the launch, thinking, One shot, make it good.

Next to my head a section of the rail exploded.

Teddy said, "Stay right there."

It was no warning shot. He'd meant to hit me.

Kate made her move. She came up at a run, holding the bang stick in both hands. I'm not sure what her plan was, or if she had one. The chance of getting close enough to Teddy was slim, made slimmer by Billy Briggs. I'm not sure what Billy had in mind, either. Maybe he just wanted the weapon for himself. Certainly he had no reason to save Teddy's life.

But that is exactly what he did. He tried to grab the stick from Kate's hands. The business end of it slid along his arm and into the base of his neck as momentum carried Kate forward. There was a popping sound, not very loud or impressive, but it was enough to kill Billy Briggs.

He didn't know he was dead, not for a moment or two. He tried to grab under his chin, like he thought maybe he could do something about the big hole in his neck and the fountain of arterial blood. He looked, as his body crumpled on the deck, like he was trying to strangle himself.

There was only the one shot in that bang stick. With the shell expended, it was just another baton, not even heavy enough to strike a solid blow. Harmless. Maybe Teddy didn't know that, or maybe he was just reacting. Whatever, he fired two quick shots into Kate Starling from a range of about ten feet.

The first shot turned her around, facing Harp, who was leaping up, trying to pull her out of the way. The second shot entered the back of her head, taking a chunk of her lovely forehead along as it exited.

Mindy screamed. I think I screamed, too, but it was the wail Harp made when he realized what had happened that put sparkles of ice in my blood. A discordant shriek of mourning and sorrow shattered the still air. It was the lonesomest sound I ever hope to hear.

Teddy saw his chance. He grabbed the winch line and slipped down it into the launch. He turned, trying to find his balance in the swaying boat, as Harp got to his feet and charged.

Firing at a moving target is tough, no matter how good you are. Firing at a moving target while you're moving—and the launch was swinging and swaying —is almost impossible. I think Harp would have made it if the little boat hadn't swung so far outboard of the hull. It was easily eight feet from the rail when he jumped.

By then Harp was airborne. Two hundred and forty pounds of grief. He cleared the rail, no problem. I think his outstretched hands just brushed the side of the launch. Then he dropped. The black seas closed over him, snuffing out his scream of anguish, and he vanished from sight.

Mindy was huddled over Kate, pounding futilely on her chest. She might as well have tried to resuscitate a rag doll.

"Get down!" I shouted, scampering to her on my knees.

She looked at me, befuddled.

I was pulling her away from Kate's body and made her hug the deck. I was expecting Teddy to finish what he'd started, but he was too busy cutting the motor launch free of the davits to waste time potting targets on a sinking vessel.

"Hear that?" I said. "He's got the engine started."

There was another, more ominous sound. The enormous sigh of water rushing into *Ducat* as her ruptured hull began to go down.

The life rafts were lashed to the observation platform, behind the bridge, at the highest level of the superstructure. We scrambled up as the hull shuddered itself free of the reef, taking great gulps of water as it went. It is a disquieting sensation, the feeling of something sinking out from under you. Survivors of earthquakes speak of similar disorientation of the senses. The feet seek that which is no longer there. The eyes misinterpret the available data, fooling the brain. There is a refusal to accept what is manifestly obvious: the center does not hold, mere anarchy is loosed upon the senses.

Ducat hit a chunk of submerged reef on her way down. The shock of it was transmitted through the hull. For just a heartbeat's worth of hope I thought she had found a shallow bottom, that the bridge deck might remain above the water. Then *Ducat*— more gallant in death than she had a right to be, given her flawed design—skidded off that last, restraining section of reef and began to slip under, bow first. Making a curtsy to the breaking seas.

One of the life rafts had been torn away. All that remained was an empty section of rail. The fiberglass pod housing the remaining raft—our only hope—was cracked. Part of the bright-yellow raft emerged like a flower attempting to blossom. The pod was lashed with half-hitches. I plucked at the knots with numb, cramped fingers and was unable to get them loose.

"Look!" Mindy shouted, pointing to a towering sea.

The cloud cover had thickened, diffusing most of the moonlight. I could just barely make out what had attracted her attention. The motor launch, steaming bravely up a mountainous wall of water. The whine of her little four-cylinder engine carried briefly. Then she was over the crest of the giant swell, skidding down into the trough, and we saw no more of her.

There was no time to consider the enormous injustice of Murray O'Shea and his mercenary killer making off with the gold. There was no time for anything but the blasted half-hitches. Submergence in saltwater had tightened the knots into mean little dacron knuckles. It was hopeless. Finally I smartened up enough to jam my hand into the cracked raft pod and root around for the knife that was bound to be included in the survival package.

Bound to be. Had to be. And of course it was. I had the knife out of the sheath and was sawing at the knots, loving the way the line split open under the fresh blade, when someone screamed.

I looked at Mindy. She looked at me.

"Paul," she said. Then shouted, "Paul! Over here! The raft!"

I am ashamed to admit I had forgotten all about the boy from Minnesota. He had elected to remain on the bridge when Harp led the rest of us below to restake his claim on the gold. Evidently he had remained there, with only dead Boone for company. Now, as *Ducat* foundered, he came out of hiding. Only his head and his clenching fingers emerged from the hatch as he struggled to climb out, fighting the momentum of the careening boat. A woeful Kilroy, lacking the necessary strength to pull himself free.

"Come on, Paul," Mindy shouted. "You can do it!"

Clearly he couldn't. The pitching deck was too much for him. He just couldn't drag himself through the opening. Weakened by storm and fear, he was reduced to a pair of big, spooky eyes and the skinny fingers gripping the hatch under his chin.

The last knot dissolved under the knife. I ripped the plastic pod apart and found the inflation mechanism. By then *Ducat*'s bow was completely submerged. Only part of the bridge and the rear observation deck remained abovewater.

"Paul!" Mindy gave me a look. I could see the resolution in her eyes. She'd made up her mind.

"Don't leave the raft," I warned.

She left the raft and went for Paul. It was dumb and stupid and brave. And like most acts of mindless courage, it was doomed. I jerked the inflation cord, made sure my hands were twisted into the lifelines, and tried to follow her, dragging the raft behind me. An equally dumb act.

Ducat, having made her curtsy, decided she'd lingered long enough. The last act was over and done, *finis*. All at once she sank like a stone, pitching me and the raft into the water. I was not really surprised to find myself on the wrong side of things. Under the water with the raft on top.

The seas, rushing in to cover the last of *Ducat*, tipped the raft over. Now I was right side up, more or less. I dragged myself inside. Then something tried to drag me back out again. I kicked my leg, trying to shake whatever it was loose. I wanted to stay in the raft. Why wouldn't it let me?

Stash!

Who he? I knew someone by that name.

"Stash!"

It was Mindy, clawing at my ankle. I grabbed the first part of her I could find, the short tufts of her hair, and dragged her aboard. Undignified, maybe, but effective. While she coughed up about a quart of seawater, I got a safety harness on her and then on myself and clipped the lines to the rungs on the raft.

There was no way to gauge the size of the seas. All I knew was, at the bottom of the trough, in the valley between swells, I could not see the crests above. And when the raft shot up, rising, finally gaining the crest and steadying itself for a moment before tipping into the steep slide down, in that giddy instant at the crest I could not see the bottom of the trough.

Nor did I want to. Our world was the raft. I had no curiosity about the turmoil outside. The sea and the whiplash end of the storm were elemental forces over which I had no power. All I could do was try to shut it out, make it go away. I managed to secure the little tentlike cover and bail out some of the water that sloshed around inside.

Mindy sat up and helped bail. "I had him," she said, hoarse from the water she'd swallowed. "I had him right in my hands and he slipped away."

"You tried."

"It's not fair," she said.

"No," I agreed, "it's not fair."

"The bastards got away with it."

I said, "Looks that way, if they make it," but my heart wasn't in it. I was too cold and wet and happy to have Mindy alive to feel the proper indignation. Also I was interested in what I had just found in one of the zip-lock survival bags.

"Son of a bitch," I said. "I should have known."

And really, I should have. The raft came equipped with an emergency radio beacon. I pulled out the antenna, activiating the broadcast mechanism. An amber light began to blink. The signal was going out. The only question, then, Was somebody listening?

22 _____

THERE ARE some who make their living on the open sea who will badmouth the U.S. Coast Guard, given half a chance. I'd been critical of the Guard myself now and then. Made disparaging remarks about dungareed farmboys employed as deckhands, the young seamen who make little effort to learn the local waters, and the officers who can't seem to take a boat under tow without fouling lines or puncturing hulls.

All of that is very small beer next to this one unalterable fact: four people who didn't know me from Adam got into a Sikorsky HH3F and took off from the Key West helipad in the middle of a killer hurricane. Their mission was to locate a radio beacon, a faint, repeating signal on the marine band. They had no way of knowing if anything alive was connected to that beacon. They went anyway, well aware they would be flying into winds that could bat their red-and-white rescue chopper through the sky like a badminton birdie. Because, as the pilot later said, it was part of the job.

Some job.

Mindy and I didn't know if anyone was looking for us. We could only hope. We were an orange speck on a black, maddened sea in the dead of night. An air rescue seemed unlikely. We would have to fend for ourselves. We had at our disposal a paddle, a compass, a flashlight, a packet of chocolate bars, a gallon of distilled water, and three hand-held flares. Did I mention the sunscreen?

"Better rub some on your nose," Mindy advised gravely. "You might get moon-burned."

"Moon is gone," I said. "The moon got the hell away while the getting was good."

"Where are we going?"

I said, "We're going up and down. Part of the time we're going sideways."

"Yeah, but which way does the compass point?"

I looked at it. "Compass points to magnetic north. It always points to magnetic north, that's what a compass is supposed to do."

"You know what I mean."

I did indeed. I still had no idea where our little raft world was headed. My guess was, wherever Celeste wanted to take us. No doubt there were an infinite number of possibilities, but only two came to mind: out to sea or in toward shore. Neither one an encouraging prospect. Shore, with the tumult of breaking surf, was probably the more lethal destination. And the most likely.

Wherever the raft was heading, there was not a damn thing we could do about it. Except make an altar of that beacon and pray to whatever saint was in charge of radio waves. The blinking amber light was some consolation. The remarkable warmth of Mindy's compact body was an even better kind of comfort.

"It's that extra thickness of subcutaneous fat," she explained, intertwining her legs with mine. "That's what makes us females so tough."

"Sub what?"

"Under the skin. More blubber."

"I wouldn't call that blubber, exactly."

"I ever mention I was a girl scout?"

"You're changing the subject."

"Not exactly. See, we learned a lot of neat stuff in the girl scouts. Like how friction makes heat."

"The old rub-two-sticks-together trick? Mindy, my dear, we haven't *got* two sticks to rub together."

She put her lips to my ear and said huskily, "We've got something better."

"Are you sure?" I said. "We're at sea in a flimsy rubber raft in the middle of a hurricane."

"Exactly," she said. "What have we got to lose?"

She had a point.

Behavioral experts will tell you that the impulse to mate is often strongest in close proximity to death. The need to reproduce is programmed into the psyche, and the program starts running when the machine is in danger. This is true of many species, not excluding the human kind.

Well, maybe. All I know is, I never felt so vital and alive as I did on that wild waterbed, not knowing from one moment to the next if we would be crushed under a collapsing wall of water. We were teasing the ghoul with the sickle, thumbing our noses at Mr. Jordan.

It was fun.

One time, after the raft had been hurtling down a crest at unnerving speed, Mindy giggled and said, "Hey, remember that old joke about feeling the earth move? Well, lover, I just felt the ocean move."

In my opinion, it's the best way to ride out a hurricane—making love and laughing at bad jokes. I was able to forget, for a while, all the should-haves that were scuttling like roaches in the back of my mind. I was able to forget myself completely. My ego had been scattered to the wind and waves, and without an ego it was impossible to experience guilt. The should-have part of me was gone, temporarily. I existed only as an extension of Mindy, a function of her pleasure. To have and to hold, to touch and to laugh.

Celeste must have approved, because she let us live. She lifted us, slammed us, rocked and rolled us, kissed us with breaking waves, shook us like peas in a pan, but when dawn broke, we had survived.

It was Mindy who first remarked on the strange light glowing through the raft cover. "Are my eyes playing tricks?" she asked. "Is that *sun*?"

I cracked open the cover just long enough to get a peek at the sky. Dawn. I couldn't see much of it through the cloud cover, certainly not the sun itself, but dawn it was. No dispute.

"What's for breakfast, Captin Queeg?"

"Portions of chocolate bar, sautéed in saltwater."

The roaring sound, when it first came to my attention, sounded like surf breaking on a distant beach. Maybe that's why I tried to ignore it. If our raft world was about to collide with reality, I didn't want to know. Let it come while we were embraced, oblivious.

Pretty soon it got too loud to ignore. We zipped open the tent and looked up to see a miracle.

A strange, wonderful figure was descending from the sky. Rather he was descending from a red-and-white helicopter. That was how we came to be rescued. A deliverance from heaven, courtesy of the United States Coast Guard.

I'd never been so glad to have four strangers drop in for a visit. Names need be mentioned: Lieutenant Jane Crosby, pilot; Lieutenant Tom Babowski, co-pilot; Steve Victor, Seaman 1st Class; and Nathan Birnbaum, Seaman 1st Class. It was Birnbaum who dropped down on that thin, swaying cable, in ninety-knot winds, to see if there was life in the orange raft.

"Didn't look like much from the air," he said when he got us aboard the aircraft. "But what the heck, we were already out there, we had to check it out."

He really did say "what the heck." Then he wrapped us in blankets and took us home.

It took three days to shovel the mud from Duval Street. The only place on Key West that hadn't been inundated by the floodwaters was Solares Hill, and that had been struck by lightning. Served 'em right, the locals said, for being so high and dry.

Mutt's bait shack ended up on Christmas Tree Island.

"You watch," he said, disgusted. "Some hippie'll be livin' in it inside a week."

"I'll help you build a new shack, Mutt."

"That's not the point."

But he couldn't say what the point was, other than that Celeste had disturbed him more than he cared to admit. The hurricane had disturbed everyone on the island, and not just the forecasters who had failed to predict it. Palm trees were stripped bare, roofs blown off, the water main was fractured, the power was out for most of a week. Boats sank in the harbor. There were tarpon on Front Street, and ospreys flying through shattered windows into luxury rooms at Casa Marina.

At the height of the storm Sloppy Joe's ran out of rum. The way I heard it, the bartenders had stood their ground, donning waders when the place flooded, but the rum shortage was a disaster not to be borne. Volunteers had formed a human chain and passed bottles over from Rick's. It was beautiful, everyone said, how a good storm brought out the best.

Most of it I heard after the fact. When the happy

shock of surviving wore off, a kind of gray, prickly glumness came over me. I decided I'd had enough of human company, and that included Mutt, although he's only about half-human. Partly it was what had happened to Harp and Kate and the boy from Minnesota. Part of it—most of it, probably—was what happened with Mindy after we got to Key West.

Granted, I'd made a fool of myself. Well, a guy is entitled to play the clown every now and then. Sometimes you just have to put on the big red nose and make silly noises with horns and pig bladders and trip over your too-big clown shoes and propose marriage.

You'll notice I stuck that in at the end. I'm not in the habit of proposing marriage. Maybe I need to take a few lessons. Maybe it was silly not to have checked with Mindy before making my little speech and uttering the fatal words.

Her first reaction was to laugh. A titter that sounded like broken crockery. Instantly the heart on my sleeve, polished and spiffed up for the occasion, shriveled up like a piece of pan-fried liver.

"Stash, honey, I'm sorry," she said. "It was wrong of me to laugh. My head's still all messed up from the storm or I never would have, honest. The problem, you dear, lovely man, the problem is I'm already married. I guess I forgot to mention that, huh?"

Hence the shrapnel in my soul. I would get over it, of course. It was just a matter of time. If you tell yourself that often enough, eventually it will be true. The wounds will heal. The ego will reinvent itself. Meanwhile, you spend a lot of time in your hammock, if you have one.

Lily and Sam came around to help clear the mud out of my bungalow. Sam found a good-sized mangrove snapper under the refrigerator and chased Lily around with it, the two of them screeching and giggling like ten-year-olds at a pajama party. That was supposed to convince me not to feel bad about all the things that had gone wrong. Like, for instance, not recovering Sam's ten grand.

"It's only money," she said. "Come on, cheer up, willya? You look like somebody died."

"Hush," Lily said.

"My big mouth," Sammie said.

I came out of my cave only twice in those early weeks after the storm. The first was when the pilot whales came back to Smathers Beach. Dr. Lauren Ashby called and so I rolled back the stone and ventured out. This time there wasn't a lot anyone could do. The whales were determined to beach themselves and no amount of pushing and shoving could dissuade them. Fifty-three whales came ashore over a two-day period and all of them perished, suffocated by their own weight.

"It just doesn't make sense," Dr. Ashby said to the reporters following the story. "I've done autopsy after autopsy and there's no pattern. If a sickness makes them do it, I can't put a name to it."

I have a theory of my own, not based on scientific expertise. Actually it is more of a feeling, an empathy for any creature that lives in the water and yet must breathe the air. I think there is something in the sea itself that compels whales to seek the land, a kind of crystal-blue persuasion as powerful and regular as the tide or the wind or the rising of the moon.

The second time I went out, it was at the request of Lieutenant Nelson Kerry.

"I think we found a couple of friends of yours," he said. "They came ashore on Bahia Honda, Atlantic side."

We drove up to Bahia Honda in his cruiser. I think

Nelly thought the trip would cheer me up, although I can't imagine why. I've never liked looking at dead people, even ones I had reason to despise.

Bahia Honda is a state park and Nelly paid the admission because he wasn't on official business, not really. The Monroe County Sheriff's Department had taken charge of recovering the bodies. Informing Kerry was simply a courtesy. We parked in the lot and walked along the dunes until we came to what looked like a beach party. There were deputies there, and park rangers, and a gentleman in a gray suit who I assumed was FBI, or one of the other alphabet outfits.

The objects of all the attention and frivolity were in the wet sand, where the tide had nudged them. Two bodies tangled together in about a hundred feet of half-inch anchor line. A week in the water does a lot of damage, and the crabs had got at them some, but there was enough left to see who they were, or rather who they had been.

The one with the rope looped around his neck was Terrible Ted. The same rope linked him to Murray O'Shea. There was a .38 automatic in Teddy's pocket, and three of the twenty-dollar gold pieces. Murray had lost his pants somehow, and his wallet along with them, but dental records confirmed his identity.

The gold pieces made quite a hit in the news. Eventually the whole story came out, about Harper King being a convicted conman and Murray O'Shea's involvement in the shady empire Fernando Del Ray left behind. *Solares Hill* ran a long investigative piece and the *Miami Herald* splashed a picture of the three recovered coins on the cover of the Sunday supplement. They quoted various experts and historians and finally concluded that it was anybody's guess who the coins had belonged to, or where they were going, or even what vessel had carried them, although there was an interesting legend about a ton of Union gold stolen from Fort Jefferson by rebels and taken away in rowboats. Treasure-hunters came from all over, scouring the length of the keys for the motor launch and the load of coins it had carried away from *Ducat*. Everyone seemed to have a theory about where the storm had taken it. Sugarloaf Key or Spanish Harbor, or into Bahia Honda Channel, or maybe back out to the reef.

That was a little more than a year ago. So far no one has found the motor launch or the gold that was in it.

I've got another theory, and this one hasn't anything to do with whales. It's based on a postcard. It found me one rainy afternoon in the Green Parrot, when I stopped in to celebrate a charter being canceled on account of the weather. I wasn't in a fishy-type mood that day, and being canceled suited me. I wanted to play sad tunes on the juke and sip a few beers and smoke the kind of cigar that would make decent people keep their distance.

Don't get the idea I was thinking about Mindy. It wasn't her, it was a lot of little should-haves, some that had come along after the hurricane had blown through and Mindy had gone back to the husband she claimed to have in Boca Raton. Anyhow, I was drinking beer and smoking a domestic cigar and trying to decide what buttons to push on the juke when the bartender leaned over the counter and handed me a postcard.

"This's been on the register for a couple weeks," he said. "You ain't been in lately, I guess."

"I guess," I said, and examined the card. On the glossy side was a snapshot of a pretty Indian girl from a tribe in the Amazon. She had gold bangles on her wrists and gold chains around her neck and a small gold ring in her nostril, very pretty and delicate. On the reverse was a Brazilian postmark and my name, care of the Green Parrot.

That was all. The space reserved for wish-you-were-here taunts was blank. It was mighty intriguing, that blankness. It meant I could think what I liked.

What I like to think, on a good day, is that Harper King didn't die at all, that somehow he got himself aboard that little motor launch, threw his two tormentors to the waves, and made it to shore with the gold. Or maybe without it. The gold doesn't really matter. I like to think he's down there in the Amazon, looking for new and bigger treasures, or maybe hawking patent medicine to the natives. Selling blue sky and daydreams and his crazy idea of hope everlasting, amen.

On bad days I know damn well that card could have been sent by anyone with the price of a stamp. But then there aren't too many bad days, not this far south.

About the Author

Before turning to fiction, W. R. Philbrick covered the waterfront as a longshoreman and later as a boatbuilder. From time to time he has lived and worked in the Florida Keys, most recently aboard the *Caribaya,* a vessel he designed and built.